Satan's Naughty List

Lexi Gray

Thank you!

Blurb

Demons don't stop chasing you. You simply stop running.
Run until you can't.
Throat raw, feet torn, the devil gives chase.
You scream and thrash, hoping for a savior...
Until not only one, but two come to the rescue.
That's far too easy.
Demon's never stop.
Physically? You can heal.
Mentally? You'll never be the same again.
Tis' the season for survivors.

What Nomad and Techy have is good. It's great, even.
Why fix something when it isn't even broken?
Enter Aspen.
Shy, reserved, and riddled with trauma.
Who would have thought that the girl with an aversion to men,
would fall in love with not only one guy, but two.
Hold onto the light because the season is filled with darkness.

Dedication

Ask and you shall receive...
Welcome to another episode of hot and steamy,
featuring your favorite male duo.
Then, add a female with a slight aversion to men...
Talk about a fast paced slow burn.
Buckle up, babies.
It's time to ride.

Trigger Warnings

DARK THEMES

Male on Male action

Vulgar Language

Violence

Bone Breaks

Blood

Near-death experiences

Suicidal thoughts

BDSM elements

Open-Door sex scenes

Off-screen Sex Trafficking, Rape & Flashbacks

Author Note

Satan's Naughty List takes place about three years after the end of Satan on Wheels. While it is the second book, it can be read as a stand-alone, but you'll better understand it if read in order.
It is *technically* a holiday special, but it's more focused on the cold season. Ish.

If you know me, no you don't.
My mental health is fine.
For the most part.

Chapter One

NOMAD

Wiping the sweat from my forehead, I feel the greasy smear left behind. A shallow curse is the only attention I give it. The grease from the chain makes my hands slippery, no matter how much I dry it on the rag. Holding tightly onto the wrench, I crank the ratchet until I can't without risking busting the bolt. Grabbing the pre-set torque wrench, I hook it up and slowly push until I hear the shallow *click*. Bolting in the fender, I take a step back.

Pride swells in my chest as I dry my hands off and admire my work. My 1947 Indian Chief is back to its original beauty. The seafoam blue mixed with the fallen brown is like a dream. I swear I can see the sun glinting off the beauty, even though it's the middle of the night.

"What are you still doing down here?" His voice sends a shiver down my spine, my cock jumping in my jeans as his fingers drag down my back. Techy lays his head on my shoulder, admiring my bike with me. Scratching my beard, I lay my head on his and give him a quick recap on my work. He listens as I complain about the fender being a bitch and needing patched due to an old rust hole.

"Either way, just look at her. She's a beauty." Admiration is clear in my voice, the girl I've been working on for months is finally complete.

"If I didn't know better, I'd think you were talking about a submissive," he chuckles, his fingers grazing the waist of my pants, right by the button. I'm not sure when it traveled to the front. I'm not going to stop him from having a good time. "Ice is laying down on the roads this time of year. You won't be able to ride it come spring."

"When there's a will, there's a way. Plus, you know better, I'll only scene with you," I coo mockingly, snapping my hand to meet his wrist when he suddenly dips it in. "Did you prep?"

"You think I'd come down here and get ready to beg without it?" He teases, shaking my grip off him. Lifting his head, he meets my eyes, that same wicked glint meeting me as it has since we got together.

"Close to five years and I still can't get enough of you," I breathe, leaning down to meet his plush lips. He doesn't hesitate, meeting me in the middle as we kiss like our lives depend on it.

"It's because my dick is too good," he quips back, tugging my bottom lip away. Fully turning my body toward him, I snatch his head by the nape of his neck, keeping his hot little body pressed against mine. We're close to the same height, but he's still just a few inches shorter than me.

"I think you'll be saying that in a few minutes when I've got you bent over this beautiful bike while I admire you both. Then I'll shove my cock so damn deep you'll taste it." Tipping his head back up, we combine forces and dominate each other. I want him to be so damn wanton before I fuck him silly. He'll be delirious when I'm done.

"Please, Nomad," he gasps as I pull back from his lips, biting down on his neck and giving him love bites. I don't draw blood, but he hisses with every bite. He knows that I love to mark him, tell everyone that he's mine. It doesn't matter if he wears my ring or has my name tattooed on his cock. I want everyone to know that he's off limits in all aspects.

"That's a good boy, begging for me," I grunt, rubbing my covered cock against his. "What do you want me to do, hmm?" Sucking his earlobe between my teeth, I let soft puffs of air cast into the shell of his ear. Reaching between us, I undo the button on my pants then the button on his. The plain cotton shirt he wears falls over my hand, letting me feel his hardened core without seeing it. The soft trail of hair that trails down to the edge of his boxers is just another tease.

"Please let me suck you," he groans as I tug his earlobe away from his body and let it roughly drag through my teeth.

"Who am I to deny my sweet husband? Pull your cock out." He does as asked, shaking like a teenager who's never gotten laid before. I think it'll always be like this between us. I just can't get enough of him. Skimming both hands to meet on his shoulders, I shove him onto his knees. His face is level with my straining erection that threatens to tear the stitches of my jeans. He fumbles to pull me free, shoving the tight denim down to my knees.

"Can I?" He asks, jaw dropping open and wetting his lips. Wrapping one fist around the base of my cock and the other in his hair, I guide his perfect mouth over me. Immediately he sucks me into his warmth, his tongue dragging over the bottom of me as I fuck into his throat. Just the way he likes it.

"Fuck, I love the way you suck my dick," I grunt, rearing back and slamming home. He groans in agreement, swallowing as I hit the back of his throat. "I bet your ass is just waiting to be filled, isn't that right? You're just a dirty boy who loves cock. Stroke yourself, Techy."

As I slide out of his mouth, the saliva stream hangs between us. With absolute fascination, I watch my man rub himself to the precipice of pleasure, then slow back down. Self-edging sucks. Cupping his jaw, I devour his lips. He tastes salty, just as I anticipated. Not that I'm complaining.

"Up," I demand, stepping back. He shuffles to stand, kicking off his bottoms the rest of the way. I'm half tempted to caveman his shirt and just rip it in half, but I hold myself back. Instead, I lift the hem and let him take it off. I admire his bare chest, free of any tattoos besides the club tattoo. He wears it proudly, not that he was given much of a choice back in the day.

"Over the motorcycle, present that hot ass to me, Pax." He does as asked, dropping onto his elbows on the seat and curving his back to push his bottom out. It's perfectly pale with a slight tan from the summer. He'd work without a shirt, get all sweaty and sun kissed...

I palm his globes, the slight glaze of blond hair doesn't faze me. It never has. He's been my rock through the worst of it all, and I'd do anything for him. Looking down, I realize he's got his plug shoved in, prepared just as he'd promised. My hands are dirty from work and it wouldn't be safe for me to work him through without cleaning them. Reaching around, I fumble in the toolbox for a moment and grab the small stashed bottle of lube. The cap pops open with a subtle sound then the cool trickle meets his swollen hole. He jumps slightly then coos when I tap the head of the plug.

"You're such a good little submissive," I coo, using my free hand to smack his ass. A yelp followed by a pleasured groan follows. The pale is now a very light shade of pink. "I wonder what it would look like red."

"Show me, daddy," he moans and wiggles. Looping my finger into the plug holder, I pull it out slowly. His tight ass releases it with a *pop*.

"You caught me at a bad time, baby. I can't stretch you out, so you're going to just have to fucking take it." I send a series of swats to his bottom, the color deepening every time.

"Yes sir," he agrees, nodding his head on the leather seat. "I can take it." The grease transfers from my hands to his ass, the globes covered in a smudges of gray, heat radiates off his skin. Notching my cock to his tight, puffy ring, I press forward as gently as I can. He jerks slightly, before relaxing and pushing back, letting me in.

Words of encouragement with a hint of degradation, I keep him on his toes as I sink deeper and deeper to the hilt. Breathing hard, the air hisses through my teeth as my balls slap against his. "Fuck, you're so damn tight." Stretching his ass cheeks apart, I slowly retreat before pushing back into his tight heat. "I love how your ass just sucks my cock in," I grunt. My hands pull back and send a unison smack on to his delicious ass.

"More, I need more," he gasps. I pick up the pace just slightly, not enough to send him over the edge. His moans and groans change tunes until I hit the spot I know drives him crazy. His short nails claw into the metal of the bike, one hand reaching back for me. Lacing our fingers together, I pin his arm behind him and drive home. The slight tingle in my spine starts, my toes curling. My free hand moves from his hip to the base of his neck, fisting his hair and drawing his body up.

"Jerk yourself off, I want your cum all over my fucking bike. Mark it, baby." His pitch turns almost squeaky as he pumps himself quickly. The bulbous head of his beautiful cock is bright red and weeping, pearls of cum slide through the slit and onto the bike. It'll be a hassle to clean later, but that's a project for another day.

My balls draw tightly into my body, and I'm sitting on the edge as we collide over and over again, his ass squeezing me for everything I have. "Cum." The command is simple but rough. His body trembles and stutters as he growls his release, coating the seat of my bike. We both observe the creamy color ooze down the metal and drip slowly. "Shit, I'm going to fill this ass so damn full of my seed, you'll fucking taste it," I grunt, moving from his hair to the front of his throat.

"Yes," he chants, over and over again as he keeps coming. Ropes of it pull from him and settle around us.

"Fuck!" I roar, slamming home as my balls draw into my body, my own stream of cum shooting deep into his tight ass.

Chapter Two

 TECHY

His shaggy hair tickles my shoulder as his chest puffs with air. Half soft already, his cum slowly drips between us. It's almost erotic, but I also know that cleaning this up is going to be a bitch. Good thing it's Nomad's job.

"I love you, Pax," he mutters, kissing the bitten marks on my neck. I swear I purr as he strokes up my ribs, squeezing the sensitive flesh that's on the brink of being ticklish. I can't help the squirming as he continues his slow movements, massaging my sore muscles. Apparently, tensing and arching your back in an odd position isn't easy on the joints or muscles.

"I love you, Drew" Tilting my head to the side, he kisses up until we lock lips, the odd angle not deterring either of us. This man has consumed me for years, but the last five have been a rollercoaster. "Gosh, I still remember when Widower caught us," I chuckle wistfully. Though it wasn't a good time then, we all laugh about it now.

"The thought makes me want to vomit every time it's brought up," he grunts, flicking my ear. A slight pout forces my bottom lip to stick out, but he's quick to suck it into his mouth. While I'd like to sit here with him growing soft, I do have things to do also.

"Speaking of Widower," I start, nudging my butt backwards to get him off. He does as silently requested, letting himself drag out and flop against his leg. "There's a case that we've been working on, something that's been kind of hush-hush."

"Is it the trafficking op?" Nodding, I help get him situated.

"Yeah, I guess a group of girls escaped. We're on the hunt for them and are trying to avoid them going back to the cartel. You're still good with doing call-outs, right?" I ask, placing my hands on his chest. The club has been tracking them for over a year, but the day the first snowfall settled, a group of girls escaped. We're hoping we can have them help us in locating the Ergot Cartel. "You know you can say no," I press, shifting my hands to clasp behind his neck. His own hands shift to my hips, cupping the slight curve.

"You don't have to worry about me. I've already told Widower that I'm prepared to take whatever steps necessary to ensure those girls are safe," he reassures, patting my butt gently. "I think the hunt starts in the morning for them."

"Hunt?" I scoff, smacking him upside the head. "We're not hunting them down, you ding-dong. That makes it scarier for them!"

"What am I supposed to call it, then?" He narrows his eyes, staring me down. As if that's intimidating. I've seen this man flay someone's tattoo off their body, stretch it across like a canvas and deliver it to another MC. If that's not scary, then I don't know what is.

"Oh, I don't know...how about a search?" I quip, the sass obvious in my voice. His eyes roll into the back of his head.

"You call it what you want, but you're not the one riding to go hunt them down," he states matter-of-factly. This is a battle I'm not going to win, so I surrender with a tender kiss.

"So, no test drives coming up?" I ask playfully. "You know, since there's literal ice on the ground." He looks shocked for a moment, pushing away from me and looking into the darkness through the windows on the garage door. I'm pretty sure I mentioned this when I came down, but he was thinking with the wrong head I'm sure. I can see past his head, small flurries casting downward outside. It's almost poetic. Almost.

"Fuck," he grumbles, crossing his arms over his broad chest. "Does that mean..." he pauses, a look of horror crossing his features as he swings to look back at me. Slapping a hand over my mouth, I hold in the giggle that I want to release.

"Oh, it sure does," I tease, slowly backing away. This man hates nothing more than... "You've gotta drive the prospect vans."

Turning on my heel, I jog out of the garage and back up the stairs. If we didn't just fuck, I'd be concerned he'd give chase. Slowing at the top, I grab my phone from my pocket and start skimming through emails from the prospects. In the most recent batch of guys, eight of them took interest in the technical side. A few of them went under the wing of the executioner while others just kind of piddle in between.

The round of men in my sector have been nothing but amazing, if I do say so myself. While I've taught them how to do things...the *right* way, they've caught on quickly. There's only one guy that I'm not so keen on, but that's a decision that Widower and Nomad will make when that time comes. I'll get a little bit of a say, then it's all them. They'll have to be able to pass based on skill, not their riding ability.

"Tee-tee!" I whirl around just in time to see my niece barrel into me. She's only just turned three, but lord have mercy. She's three going on thirteen with that attitude.

"Careful, 'Phelia!" Hudson calls, chasing after the rugrat. He's got another chest carrier where their infant lays. Looking around, I don't see my nephew running around anywhere.

"Where's Axel?" I ask, scooping the toddler into my arms and cooing at her. She's the world's cutest kid, I swear. I may be biased because all three of them are freaking adorable, but still.

"He's with his mom hunting those girls. Something about wanting to learn the ropes." Hudson gives a lax shrug, petting the baby on the head. He nuzzles Sebastian's little head, probably absorbing that sweet baby scent. I love babies, but I want to be able to give them back once they've gotten on my nerves.

"You know where they went? I think I've got an update." He gives me detailed directions on where she is, as if I've not lived in this club house for several years. Instead, I nod along and pretend to actually be listening.

Before I got bombarded with a kid, I received an email with the potential whereabouts of a few girls. We've got guys scouting now, but the night shift has double the men as the day crew. According to the prospects, there may be a reward for the girls to '*be returned safely*'. In other words, it's a bounty to get the girls back to their handlers.

I shudder with Ophelia in my arms, cradling her tightly. Trying to imagine this tiny, delicate little girl in the arms of those monsters makes my blood fucking boil. If anyone can find these girls, it's our guys. While we may be morally fucked up, we are all on the same page. Women and children are *not* to be fucked with. Unless they're in patches, of course. Then they're free game.

My phone blares in my pocket. Reaching in, I smirk. Speak of the queen and she shall manifest. "Widower! What do I owe the pleasure?" I ask, settling the squirming child down. She doesn't need to hear the shit we talk about. Innocent ears and all.

"We've got one on the north side, she's pretty banged up. She's cowering away from everyone, even me," Widower sighs. I can hear faint whimpers in the background, my heart tugging harshly in my chest. "We didn't bring the van because we weren't really looking. Came back from a drop and saw her on the side of the road. Can you assist?"

"You've got it," I assure, waving bye to Hudson and the kids. "Any other updates for the missing women?"

"There's a gang of thugs on the south side that rounded up a group of girls. They're willing to keep them safe for a pretty Franklin. Grab cash before you send a crew. I'll forward the details."

"Sounds like a plan." Putting the phone on speaker, I inform her of the email, giving her the rundown on what it contains. She curses the men who can't keep it in their pants, curses men in general, then curses only men who are douchebags. Since, you know, I've got a cock too.

"Send your coordinates, I'll be there soon," I respond, hanging up without another word. What a start to a holiday season.

Chapter Three

Aspen

"We're not here to hurt you," her voice calls, it's soft with an edge in it. My feet hurt from the run, my lungs threatening to seize as I move. My thighs are barely covered with the oversized shirt I stole, but it keeps the essentials covered, no less.

Twigs snap under me as I scour through the trees, the sharp edges on the small branches pushing splinters deeper into my skin. Ice is mixed into slush as I'm chased. I may be depleted of any sort of nutrients, but adrenaline may as well be my source right now. I can't remember the last time I'd eaten anything that wasn't just slop or had a capsule of poison stirred into it.

They can't get me.

I can't let them.

I won't risk it.

"Please leave me alone," I whimper quietly. A few entwined branches slow me down. Scaling them, I realize they're a lot more slippery than they look.

"Don't!" One of them shouts. They can't catch me. The shouts of men can be heard for miles, but I don't care. I get higher and higher. My feet scramble below me to gain traction, the moss giving away the higher I get. Their grumbling fades as I move, sliding around with each branch I scale. Stepping on a thinner branch, it gives.

I drop several inches, the force of air billowing the shirt slightly as my foot is shoved into a hole. I hear it before I feel it. A raging inferno roars in my bone as I fall backward, the shirt covering my eyes as my ankle breaks and holding me up. I dangle in silence, the urge to scream is swallowed by my will to live. I have to get out of this, I can't let them get me. I won't survive it.

"Shit, she's caught!" Another harsh voice calls. I flinch as a hand touches my shoulder, and I thrash. Nothing else makes sense besides survival. If I can dislodge myself, I can run. I can slam my bone back into place and run. "Woah, easy girl, I'm not going to hurt you," he says, his tone softening.

It's a trick, a ploy to get me to surrender. I refuse.

Another sharp snap shoots through my ankle, into my foot and up my leg. I can't feel my toes, the freezing air helping with the pain. Tricking ice drops down my leg toward my bare crotch before I'm falling again. The hard ground is further than it looked as I slam into the soil, a pained and restrained groan pushing free from my lungs. Taking a moment to gather my bearings, I see several figures approach me. Hands high like a surrender, they form a circle.

I have to get out before they can stop me...

I scream.

A blood curdling, horror show scream.

They flinch and step back in shock, giving me enough time to raise my leg and slam it on the ground, setting the bone where it *hopefully* should be. Blood pounds in my ears like a white water tides, but I know from their flinches that it probably didn't sound good. A few gagged sounds surround me, but I pay them no mind. If they vomit, that slows them down. Dropping forward onto my hands, the skin catches on rough edges below them. Like a runner on a starter block, I take off.

Adrenaline surges through my veins as I dodge man after man, shouts ringing around me as they tumble to catch up. They're all double, if not triple, my size. I slink through knocked-down trees, holes between the roots and the trunk. My heart hammers in my chest as my head grows light from the lack of food. I can't run forever. I just have to run long enough.

Risking it all, I swivel my head behind me to see three men chasing me down, their hands outstretched and ready to catch me. I turn to look ahead just in time to miss a low hanging branch.

"Shit," I hiss, my balance becoming uneven, the sudden overwhelming pain enveloping my leg as I stumble to the unforgiving earth. The men behind me are still running full speed, barely registering that I'm below them as they pound over me, falling into a dog pile above me. One of them smashes into my skin, the *snap* of the bone loud enough for me to hear over the rushing in my head.

I can't hold the agony any longer, the overwhelming understanding that I'm going to go back. No matter how much I run, I can't escape them. I feel nothing besides the burning inferno that is my leg as they move off of me. My body is smashed into the ground, my head cradled by a rock as I focus to stay awake.

I can't give up like this. I won't.

I can't.

"Please leave me alone," I sob, crawling backwards. It takes the rest of my strength to move the weight of my leg, the feeling lost in my foot all together. "Don't take me back there, please." My begs go unheard as the three men circle me, keeping me in place as one of them puts a phone to his ear.

He doesn't listen to me. None of them do. The story of my fucking life. "Just fucking kill me or let me kill myself," I scream, thrashing in a final effort to get them to back off. Before I can even blink, my arms drop. My body is like a heavy sack as my head clobbering on a sharp point, dulling the rushing around me.

"She's...I won't...it's not..." his words are muffled as a shaking hand touches my cheek. I can't even flinch. I don't know what to even do anymore.

Maybe if I let myself go...

"We're...she's not...too much blood..." the guys huddle around me, their blurry figures taking off articles of clothing and pressing them tightly around me. A whimsical giggle leaves me as I think about the times where my parents would fuss over me just like this. How they'd see a slight scratch and act as if I'd almost died.

Who would have thought that they were the ones who sold me into this?

Taps against my frozen face force me to focus. Squinting through the flakes on my eyes, I see a really cute guy. His face is gentle, not like the rest of them who all look about ready to eat me alive.

You still can't trust him.

Shaking my head, I turn to look the other way, my neck cracking as I move. The cold is fusing itself into my joints, my bones. It's easier to let the ice pound over me and freeze me into the earth. I've read about death by freezing.

You'll warm up eventually.

The same guy who tapped me earlier takes my chin between his fingers and rolls my head back toward him.

"What do you want?" I ask, though it sounds like I'd have a gallon of rum by the slur in my voice. Sike, it's just death knocking at my door.

"You. Safe." His voice is stern, but there's a sort of...pliance to it that makes me almost weak at the knees. Well, if I were standing. Maybe if it were several years earlier, I might have trusted him to take me on a date. That's one thing I'll never do again. They've fucked me up in ways that I can't even begin to breathe about.

"Let me go," I whimper, my fingertips slowly going from freezing cold to warm. It's like a slow takeover of my body.

It's happening.

"No can do." He turns to the men, calling out orders that whiz above me. There's nothing I can catch, they talk too fast for me. "Up," he barks, and my body floats.

It's an odd feeling, being this high up. The trees are missing almost all of their leaves, but the branches are covered in ice and frost. Comparing it to those old, black and white movies, we move slow enough for me to admire the darkened sky. There are no stars, just a forest painted in the night.

Blinking, my head feels heavy and my eyes feel droopy. The cold ground has nothing on this floating shit. The world could own me, yet I'd never give up the feeling right now. My brain can't connect with my fingers nor my toes. It's like they're moving, but none of them even so much as twitch.

That's a good sign for me. I fought long enough to hit the brink. Now I just need to stall for me to slip past the edge.

"Wait," I breathe, tilting my head so it drops from their hold. They stop, fumbling to keep me from going down. Parts of me slip through their big hands, dangling before they're grabbed again. I should have felt them grappling with my fucked up leg, but I feel nothing.

Exactly how I like it.

"Look over there," I whisper, using my eyes to motion. If I can get them to stall long enough...

"We're out of time," he grumbles above me, pushing hair out of my face.

"It's perfect," I mutter, my eyes rolling back as white static consumes me.

Chapter Four

TECHY

"**F**uck! We're losing her!" Picking up the pace, we hustle to get her fragile body back to the van. It's far worse than Widower made it out to be, that's for fucking sure. "Why did no one think to tell me that her leg is practically shattered?" A heavy weight in my chest pushes us faster, the guys struggling to keep up. She ran pretty fucking far with no resources and three huge executioners chasing her. Not only that, but her bone was sticking out of her leg until she managed to set it. Don't ask me how she managed that because I'm fucking clueless.

All I know, is she's fucking good.

"It wasn't like that until she climbed the stack on the south," Razor grunts, keeping her leg stable as we reach the top of the hill. "We tried to stabilize her then, but she set her own fucking leg."

"She did that?" I question, looking back at her covered, mangled leg. Her tiny body is covered in a simply black shirt, one that isn't meant for the cold winter months. From the suspected location of the warehouse she escaped to here...that's almost two weeks in running full speed. She would have needed a ride to get this far. If that's the same place, of course.

"It was gruesome, man." He shivers roughly, his skin a slight grayish color. "She didn't even make a sound when she did it. We all just about threw up," he says on a gag. Finally cresting the hill top, the crew gets to work in preparing an area for her in the van.

"Where's doc?" I call, glancing around the area. The area is lit up with headlights, though the darkness threatens to shroud us.

"She's setting up shop at the club house," Razor responds, gently settling the girl on the makeshift gurney.

"I'll patch in the girl's condition." Pulling my phone, I dial Doc Solla. She answers immediately, neither of us bothering with basic formalities as I run her through what I can see.

"Alright, what all do you have in your go-bag?" She questions, calling orders on her end.

"The only thing I have that would be of any use is a splint kit that we'll use for the drive and a bag valve." Pointing at the bag, I get Razor started on the wraps.

"That should work for now. Drive and work, if she's lost as much blood as you've described, we're running out of time." Hanging up, orders are barked from all angles. Widower is running her own task force as we rally the van.

"Let's go!" I shout, hopping into the back and slamming the door shut. Razor, Clubby and I get to work on stabilizing her condition. Placing the mask on her mouth and nose, I feel a pulse. It's faint, but there.

"She might jump." Is all the warning I get before they reposition her leg. The girl hardly shudders before falling limp again. That's not good. Razor moves around, setting her leg in his lap so it's elevated.

"ETA?" I shout, pushing air into her system.

"Less than five." The three of us in the back grumble in protest, but if we go any faster, there's a higher chance of drifting into a ditch.

"Flurries are coming down pretty heavy, Techy," the prospect calls back, fishtailing slightly on a patch of ice. We're thrown around, clawing at the bare metal to get a grip. "Shit, you guys good back there?"

"Yeah!" Clubby grunts, keeping a tight grip on the girl. Repositioning himself, he's got her head in his lap now, yanking the bag valve from me. "You can do a facial scan while she's with the doc, right?"

Looking at the girl, her dark hair is knotted and tangled, probably from months of not having the proper care. There's dark black circles positioned directly under her eyes and in the hollows of her cheeks. Her complexion is damn near translucent, most likely from the lack of sun she'd gotten while in captivity. With the advanced technology, I have no doubt I'll be able to get a hit on her. As long as she's registered in the database.

"Boss?" Looking up, both guys have narrowed eyes and furrowed brows. Shaking my head, I nod.

"Yeah, I should be able to." They don't look convinced, but there's nothing more I can say. Doc is amazing when it comes to wounds and battle incidents.

"I need more gauze," Razor hisses as blood starts pooling around his fingers and dripping down. The prospect in the front passenger seat throws a roll of that wrap up shit and a few sealed things of gauze. I work to tear out the squares as we start swapping the bloody ones.

There's a lot. The discarded ones are soaked and dripping onto the cold metal. I swear I can hear each drop hitting the flooring.

"Boss?" Snapping out of the red hazed trance, Razor moves the girls shirt up a bit more.

"Woah," I start, only to catch sight of something inked on her upper thigh. "What's that?" Leaning in closer, I realize it's a symbol. Touching the spot, it's hot and swollen, obviously pretty new.

"It looks like the cartel symbol, but I can't say for certain," Clubby mutters, squinting to see it as he pumps air.

"Turn!" We don't have time to brace as we skid around a corner, coming to a complete stop. Peering out the front, I see the drive to the clubhouse. The two prospects jump out, assisting with the doors as we shuffle around the back.

"It's going to hurt no matter what we do. Just go for it." Razor and I glance at one another before I haul her into my arms bridal style. My chest constricts as she shivers against me, her head almost snuggling into my shoulder as we run toward the house. Barging in, I can't help the way my heart hammers against my sternum. She's too light in my arms, too small. Yet, she fits perfectly. Too damn perfect.

Her matted hair is dull from dirt and oil, yet I can't help but think she's still one of the most beautiful people I've seen. She's got this angelic glow to her.

"What happened?" Nomad calls, trailing behind us. Snapping from my thoughts, I open my mouth, but nothing comes out. If I had a solid answer, I'd tell him. Unfortunately, I only know the tailend of things. Taking the steps carefully to not fall with her, I take her to the basement where Doc is set up.

"That's bad," she says, helping me lay the girl flat on her back. Once settled, Doc looks over the girl, finally reaching her face. Doc pales, jaw falling slack. "Holy shit." Razor, Nomad and I wait with bated breath. After a moment, she kicks into action. Drips are started for pain meds, sedation and antibiotics. It's a blur as she scrubs in, naming devices that I'm not familiar with. A few other prospects burst through the door, shoving us out of the way as they start prepping the girl.

"I need to be with her," I call, pushing back against them. Something in me says that I can't leave her. She needs us with her. Needs to know that we're here for her.

"No, you need to let us do our job," Doc calls, pausing with the clothing scissors. "Give the girl some damn privacy." Finally backing away, I can't get my feet to finish going the last little bit. A hand lands on my shoulder, pulling me backward.

"She knows her?" Nomad finally asks, forcing me to take the final step out of the room. A prospect shuts it and locks it, signifying that we'll have to wait to know anything more.

"I don't know," I mutter, shock coursing through me. It's hard to say what she knows, but she won't tell us right now. I trust Nomad or Widower to get the information out of her.

Looking down, my body is covered in her blood. My jacket is dripping onto the tile floor, a puddle of the girl's blood pooling beneath me.

I can't dwell on it. For now, I'll go clean up and hope Doc will open up in a little while to let me do my scans.

Chapter Five

NOMAD

My husband shucks off my hands, spins on his heels and goes back up the stairs. His face is solid white, like he'd seen a ghost. Shit, maybe he had. I stare after where he disappeared up the steps, taking two at a time.

When he was asked to go, I wanted to stop him. He's not used to the blood shed and torture of the club. While we're the brawn of the group, Techy and his crew are the brains. The club trusts him to keep us safe from the confines of the house, none of them wanting to sacrifice the guy who can make their digital footprint go away.

"He okay?" Widower appears out of thin air, eyeing the puddled spot where Techy was just standing. The only way down here is the stairs. I don't know how I missed her. "I'd think he wasn't with the way he flew past me up the stairs. Damn near knocked me over," she laughs, shaking her head.

"No, he wasn't okay," I mutter, moving my stare back to the door. The way he cradled her, refusing to leave her side. He's never acted like this toward women. We've introduced them into our bedroom in the past, but he's never done that. Never acted...territorial about them.

It's shocking, to say the least.

"What's wrong?" She questions, nudging me with her shoulder. Sighing heavily, I scrub my hands over my face. The late hour doesn't help the exhaustion we all feel. It's been a long month, let alone night. Tracking down these girls, making deals, sealing down the cartel...we're all weary.

"Drained," I huff, a dry chuckle echoing from my lungs. She laughs with me, a slight nod to follow.

"I know what you mean. Plus, add the damn Ergot bitches. Are we any closer on accessing their servers?" Glancing over our shoulders to where Techy made his swift exit, I sigh. As much as I don't want to bother him, it's a valid question. One we don't have time to wait for an answer on.

"I'm not sure. I'll check with him then call in later?" Taking a few steps back, I briefly glance at the shut door. There's light shuffling from what I can hear, machines beeping as time slowly eases by.

"How about you just let me know for Church tomorrow, yeah?" Nodding, she gives me a clap on the back, hand trailing to squeeze my shoulder. "You should have seen him out there. Like a natural. He'll be alright, just needs time." Giving her a less-than-reassuring smile, I trudge up the steps.

Some of the guys are debriefing with beers and jacket pickers, pounding the females into the vinyl countertop. Others are walking around, wishing their goodnights to the guys. It's a hit or miss, but tonight I'm in no mood to have a beer.

I just want to curl up around Techy, cuddle him closely and figure out what's on his mind. When he walked away, his shoulders were slumped heavily, his brain was obviously foggy with emotions he didn't know how to express.

Our bedroom door is slightly ajar, silence on the other side. Pushing it open, the hinges creak. Techy sits on the bed, his head perched in his hands. He doesn't even acknowledge me as I walk into the room and sit next to him. My hand lands on his back, and even then, he doesn't move.

"What's going on?" I ask gently, leaning my head on his shoulder. He gives a mirthless laugh, gripping his hair tightly.

"I don't even know. Seeing her like that...I don't know how you do it." Nodding, I rub his back soothingly. It's not an easy job, that's for sure. Especially having to hunt down women and get them to safety before some other bastard grabs them for the reward money.

"I do it because of this. The outcome. I won't have you there when we kill the sick sons of bitches that hurt those girls, but you might be there to help retrieve the girls." He sighs heavily, raking his hands through his hair before popping his head up.

"Seeing that gorgeous girl that was beaten up? What if I'm drawn to them all like this?" His eyes catch mine with earnest fear. "This pull I feel to the girl in the basement...do you feel it?" He asks, tears welling in his soft eyes. Moving my hand onto his shoulder, I bring him closer.

"You got trauma bonded to her, Pax. You're not stupid or weak for feeling it. I think it'd be a good idea to keep your distance, though." I hate that I don't even want him near her. She's gorgeous, even with the matted hair and blood stained body. Her face was shallow and distraught, and yet, she's still stunning. He leans away, shaking his head.

What if he likes her more? Leave me for her?

"I don't know if I can..." he admits softly, turning away from me. I try to pull him back into me, but he's up and out of my reach before I can. "I feel the same pull I felt toward you." Now that's an admission. My chest constricts, my throat tightens. Am I losing my husband?

"Pax, what are you saying?" I choke out, my own eyes threatening to tear up. His face is pure distress, a mix between shock and hurt.

"I'm saying that I wouldn't be closed off to opening our relationship for her...you think I want to leave you?" He asks, his voice hollow in a heartbreaking tone. "We've been together for almost five years, married almost four, and you're concerned that I'm going to leave you? I don't ever remember giving you an inkling of doubt before." He's devastated. We're both just in shock.

"No, that's not," I pause, flying off the bed toward him. He takes a step back, holding up his hand. I feel my insides crumble. "Pax, please," I beg, reaching toward him. He paces quickly, his wedding band catching in his hair as he rakes it roughly.

"I've said that I feel something for the girl. Nowhere in my words did I say I wanted to leave you." A lone tear drips down his check, my stomach sinking as I feel like an utter ass. "Are you wanting to go? Is this a sense of projection?" He sobs, his fists gripping tightly on his roots.

"No!" I bark, storming him and not giving him the opportunity to back away. Grabbing his shoulders, I force him to meet my gaze.

"You're my *everything*, Paxton Bradley. How would you feel if I suddenly asked to be open?"

"Andrew," he sighs, placing his strong hands on my cheeks. Leaning forward, he kisses me softly. It's not one based on dominance like usual. No, this kiss is claiming. He's claiming me all over again. Pulling back, he licks my bottom lip and tugging it between his teeth. Letting it snap back into place, we stare. "I understand what you're telling me. It's not something I would be open to right away either. But, I feel this...*pull*. My brain can't wrap around it. It's something deep within my gut that's telling me she is ours. *Ours.* Maybe it's a trauma bond. Probably because she almost died in my arms. Yet, I can't let that deter me. If you were there...would you not feel anything at all?"

My mouth opens then shuts almost immediately. I don't know what to say. Did I feel something when I saw that girl? Yeah. I felt awful for the shit she went through. That poor woman went through hell and back for men who only wanted her as a toy. Do I feel more though?

"No, I don't," I sigh. His face drops, taking another shift backward. "I won't lie to you, baby. You know I won't."

"I just need a minute." Turning on his heel, he quietly slips into the bathroom and shuts the door. The faint click tells me that he's locking himself in there.

"Fuck!" I roar, slamming my fist against the wall. I can't fucking win. My own husband doesn't even want me anymore.

Chapter Six

TECHY

T ears track down my cheeks, my heart constricts in my chest as I release a quiet sob. The sun is starting to rise, snow still falling heavily. Checking my phone, it's past six in the morning. Exhaustion from everything is finally hitting me as I sit on the closed toilet, sobbing into a towel to keep myself silent. Nomad didn't chase after me. He didn't even stop me from walking away. Does he just not care about our marriage anymore? He acts as if I *want* to have feelings for another. I've never even been with a woman before. Being gay is a part of who I am, who I always was.

Sniffling, I tilt my head to look at the ceiling. It'll be okay. This is just one of those rough patches that we'll get through, just like we always do. Starting the shower, I realize my hands are still covered in blood. My clothes are dried from the muddy slush of the snow. I can't imagine what the path in the forest looked like in the daylight.

A timid knock echoes through the bathroom. Before I can think, I whip the door open to see my husband standing there, hands shoved in his pockets. We always shower together, an excuse to 'conserve water'. Neither of us move as we stare, his cheeks look almost exactly like mine. Tear stained and red.

"I'm sorry," he chokes, keeping his head lowered, eyes on the ground. "You've never made me doubt before. Never. I just...you're the love of my life. I don't think I'd be able to do this life without you."

Grabbing the front of his shirt, I yank him into me. Our lips smack together in a dirty kiss, the kind that forces you to unleash everything. He attempts to pull back, but I reach around his body, fist the back of his shirt, and tug him flush against me. He grunts, stumbling slightly. While he's a bit bigger than me, I know how to handle this burly man. Using my free hand, I grasp his thick beard, forcing his lips back to mine.

"Fuck," he growls. Before I can react, I'm being slammed against the wall. His tattooed hand grasps my throat and squeezes the sides as his other hand fingers my belt loops. Teeth graze my throat, air meets the wet spot and sends a cool shiver down my back as I struggle to think. My hand is still embedded behind his back. Migrating it down, I grip his tight ass. Squeezing, I moan against him.

I have to show him I'm not going anywhere.

"You're mine," he grunts. His jean covered cock roughly rubs against mine. It's rough, his hips push, shoving against my erection as it threatens to bust the seams.

"I'm yours," I assure. "You're also mine." He grunts in agreement. Teeth gnash, lips bust, jeans get pulled off.

"Get your ass in the shower." Shoving me into the wall harshly, my head bangs as he steps back. I don't hesitate as I step behind the fogged glass.

He would absolutely tan my ass if I didn't do as he demanded. Warm water cascades down from the waterfall attachment, hammering on my tight muscles. Coiled harshly, the water soothes away the tenseness in my body. The toll of the day finally settling after everything. Looking at my feet, pink filth is pushed off me, cleansing away the physical reminder of what I witnessed. Unfortunately, it's the mental shit that I won't be able to get reprieve from.

My head tips back, eyes falling shut as I let the droplets run down my face, washing away any traces of external sadness. I know my hair is crusty with blood, the light streaks turned pink from the incessant grabbing and pulling. The sliding door opens again, still, I keep my head facing toward the ceiling. It shuts quietly, the gentle click of the latch closing. Bare, calloused hands drag up my body. My muscles clench, my jaw ticking as I force myself to not look at him.

I love my husband more than anything, yet I can't even bring myself to see his eyes. The disappointment that's going to reflect right back at me. Sighing, I turn my back toward him and reach for the shampoo.

"Here," he mutters, grasping my shoulder to stop me. His large frame steps around me, cock hardened and waiting for attention. Rolling my eyes up his body, his face shows the opposite of disappointment. Bottom lip tucked between his teeth, hands lathering soap, and his eyes hold copious amounts of desire. If his dick wasn't the tell, the whirlpool is his deep blues would absolutely be my demise.

"Turn," he rumbles, a soapy hand grasping my shoulder. Doing as I'm asked, my front is exposed to the water as he works my hair from behind me. His short nails dig into my scalp, sweeping through the strands of crusted blood. Opening my eyes, I can see the pinkish lather slipping down the walls next to me.

"It's not always that bad, Pax," he mutters, turning me around again. "Rinse." Complying, I reach up and scrub my hair free of the cleanser.

"You're used to it. I didn't want to be a blood catcher. You can agree that I'm more useful behind a computer." Huffing, I look up at my husband. He stares down at me harshly, brows furrowed in concentration.

"I would agree that you're much more useful in my bed," he grunts, pushing his hips forward. "I'd be lying if I said the dried blood look wasn't doing it for me." I can't help the laugh that bubbles out of me.

"Drew," I sigh, shaking my head. I open my mouth, but two fingers are shoved in it.

"Suck," he demands, pushing them further. Swallowing so I don't choke, I lap at his bitter fingers. "You're done talking. It's only going to lead to a session where you say you're not worth it or some bullshit. You know better than that. So, I'll just have to show you again how much you mean to me. If you want a degradation session, fine. Now, wet those fingers for me, dirty cock whore." Moaning around his digits, I let him work them in my mouth, dragging more saliva from me.

My lids threaten to shut, but his other hand wraps around my throat tightly. Balls growing heavy as my cock hardens between us, Nomad's hips shift as he plants his erection against mine. They rub aggressively, the water creating an odd friction that I'm definitely not against.

His fingers pop out of my mouth, saliva dragging with them as he rubs them over my nipples. "Shit," I hiss, bumping forward to rub against his cock.

"That's right, dirty boy. You're going to be a good little cum whore for me, right?" He grunts, reaching between us and wrapping his big hand around us both.

"Yes," I gasp as he runs his fingers over our slits, dipping his finger in slightly. Jerking, he laughs while an involuntary whimper escapes me.

"You'll do more than that." His tight grip latches around me, pumping me to full length. "I love this cock." Pearly white teeth meet me before he pulls me forward by my throat. Lips gnashing together, he practically devours me. Biting, sucking, licking, he works my mouth as his hand rubs me toward climax.

"Stop," I grunt, trying to pull away. He smiles against my mouth, head shaking slowly.

"Is that your safe word?" He whispers, kissing down my throat as his fist constricts my length. Holding me solid against him, the question hangs in the balance between us, his breathy kisses skate over my throat. I don't want him to stop. Stopping him would be the biggest edging he's ever given me.

If he's willing to have me like this, then I'm not going to be the one to stop him.

"No, sir," I retort. Straightening, he looks into my eyes.

"Good boy." He smacks my ass before taking a step back. "I want you showered, prepped and on the bed in ten minutes. If you're not there, ass up and waiting for me, you're in for a punishment."

Chapter Seven

NOMAD

I've never seen him finish a shower so quickly in my life. By the time I start on my hair, he's pushing out and drying off. Laughing, I scrub off the grime of the day. Instead of just having motor oil, I'm also covered in blood from my husband and the runaway girl.

Since the previous day, Techy and I have been awake for almost twenty-four hours. While I want nothing more than to bunker down in the sheets and snuggle my man, I need to show him that I'm serious. He's not going anywhere.

"You'd better be presenting to me," I shout, my voice bouncing off the tiles. A muffled response is yelled in return. There's no doubt that his ass is in the air, waiting for me to pound him into the next year. Bubbles swirl into the drain as I allow my stress to wash away. I need to be in the right headspace to care for my husband.

After one last rinse, I shut the water off and towel dry quickly. I can't place whether there's been a previous disconnect between us. He's not mentioned anything before today, but I'm determined to keep him where he needs to be. With me. Pushing the door open,

Techy is exactly where I told him to be. Pale and high in the air, his peachy ass wiggles slightly as I step closer.

Face stuffed into the bed, his cock is hard with those heavy balls hanging between his legs. His tight hole clenches in anticipation. Bare and clean, my mouth salivates at the picture perfect image in front of me. Pax is the perfect husband, that's for damn sure.

Kneeling on the bed, I shuffle to him, my palms skim over his ass, and he huffs in annoyance at my lack of touch. He squirms against me, almost as if he's trying to scoot backward.

Rearing back, I slap his pale bottom so hard it leaves a slight welt. He yelps into the sheets, his fists curling into the material.

"Did I say to move?" I grunt, soothing the redden skin.

"No sir," he whimpers.

"That's a good boy," I coo. My cock notches itself at his entrance, not moving as beads of pre-cum dripping onto him. Grazing over, I grip the soft cheeks in my hands and stretch him out, looking at his glorious hole.

"I can't wait to stuff this tight ass." Growling, I lean over his back and shove two fingers into his mouth again. He doesn't hesitate to lap at them like it's my cock. Cheeks hollowing, tongue swirling. Using my free hand, I grab the bottle of lube situated next to him. Popping it open, I let generous amounts of it dribble on his hole.

My fingers are soaked as I yank them out of his mouth, using the hot warmth to stretch him open and work in the lube. A mewl falls from his plush lips as I push knuckle deep.

"More, please," he whines. He trembles slightly, obviously trying his hardest to keep from getting another punishment.

"I do love to hear you beg," I tease, pushing a second finger in. Another deep groan escapes him as I rock forward to stretch him out.

"Your cock is weeping for my tight ass," he mutters, the words blurred by the sheets. "I want your thick cock shoved inside of me." I groan at his dirty words. Instead of pushing myself in, I grab the back of his neck, yank him onto his hands, and bring him for a dirty kiss. His saliva drips onto his chest from my finger fucking, but I don't give a shit.

"You want my cock? Is that it?" I growl, using my free hand to fist myself. I coat my tip in the lube that drips off his ass. "I know what you want. You want my cum shoved so far up your ass, you can taste it. That's what you want, huh?" I tease. I shove the head of my cock into him, his tightness sucking me into me. We both release a hiss in unison, mine from how he swallows me and his from the stretch. Letting go of his head, I wrap my hand around his throat, squeezing the sides just the way he likes it.

"Yes, please give me your cock," he yelps, face landing back in the pillows. "Oh, *god*." Pushing myself a bit further, the pitch of his cries gets higher. Irritation spikes in my veins. He knows I don't like when he calls for another entity.

"God doesn't exist here, baby," I scold, slamming myself all the way to the hilt. He collapses with a silent scream, mouth open and throat bobbing against my hand. "That's it, your tight ass sucks my cock in so nicely."

"You're so big," he groans, shoving sheets between his teeth. Retracting with an animalistic snarl that I didn't realize I was capable of making, I rip the material out of his mouth. His jaw snaps shut with the surprise force.

"I want to fucking hear you." Pulling my hips back, I snap them quickly in and out, not giving him time to breath.

"Yes, yes, *yes*," he chants over and over again as I brutally plow into his ass. The heat pushes me closer and closer to the edge as I force myself to hold off.

Heaving a deep breath, I send another series of blows to his ass, his skin effectively, and finally, turning bright pink. It's hot to the touch with several imprints laid before my eyes. His hips start gyrating, hands trembling as he seeks more.

"Please, sir," he croons. Eyes shut tightly, brows furrowed deeply, and a sweat bead coursing down his tones face. He's blissed out. Pulling out, I shuffle backward and sit on my heels.

He rolls onto his back, already knowing that I want to watch him as he takes his pleasure. Dropping to my elbows, I take his weeping cock in my mouth. He's on the thinner side, but he's long. His cock sinks to the back of my throat easily as I hollow out my cheeks. Clenching the sheets again, his knuckles are white with the effort needed to not touch me.

Pulling back, I smirk. "Take what you want from me, but you're not allowed to cum unless I'm inside of you." Without hesitation, his fingers grip the roots of my hair, guiding me back onto his length as I work him over. Using my elbows, I prop myself and give him the necessary room to do what he loves. Fuck my throat. His knees bend slightly as I swallow him down, and he lets himself free. Balls slap my throat as he thrashes from below me, grunting as he holds me still.

We all know the trick. They have to think they're in control every once in a while.

I watch his face through bleary eyes, waiting for his brows to do a certain wiggle, his plush lips popping open on a low rasp before I pull away. Strands of slick follow me as I disconnect. He wants to protest, I can absolutely see it, but he doesn't. Oh no, instead, he wipes the remaining saliva from my mouth and drags it onto my cock. He rubs it in, working me back to the brink. A quick slap to the hand pushes him away.

Propping back up to his entrance, he watches me with narrowed eyes. My cock sinks into him with little effort, already well used from the pounding. I wrap my hand around his length and it jerks, obviously ready to blow any moment. His arms throw themselves around my neck, nails digging into my shoulders.

"Fuck your fist," I groan, slowly removing myself from his ass before plunging back in. Each withdrawal is methodical and gentle. Then, I slam into him enough that he almost screams. He grips his cock tightly with one hand. His nails stay stuck in my neck, and I swear he's going to draw blood. Wrist rolling, his eyes roll to the back of his head then focus back on me. The head of his dick is bright red, suffering from a case of feeling left out. Cupping his balls, I roll them in my palm as I ramp up my pace, feeling my own get heavier as they draw into my body.

The tingle starts low in my body, working from my toes up my legs and through my spine. "Eyes open," I demand, watching as they were just about to slide shut. They pop open, Pax forcing them to keep from closing. "Cum." The command is simple, yet it does the job as ropes of his release land on his stomach in messy lines. His body quakes, legs shake as he shouts. His eyes are blissed out as he keeps them locked on mine. Free hand stuck in my shoulder, he grapples with my body to hang on, dragging his short, sharp nails through my skin. Hissing, I lean down and capture his plush lips on mine in a nasty kiss, biting his bottom lip. My own release detonates from me when he digs his nails into my ass.

"Paxton!" I shout. Hips stuttering against his, I can't help the moan as I blow inside of him. I stay buried inside of him as I let go. If he didn't know it before, it's my own version of marking him. This just solidifies that he's not going anywhere. "You're mine, do you understand me? You don't get to even think about leaving me. I love you more than I need air." He nods breathlessly, bringing his legs to wrap around me completely. We collapse into a pile of limbs, kisses getting placed wherever we can reach.

"I love you more than anything, Drew." Capturing my lips in a sweet kiss, we don't ravish one another. No, we take it slow. Steady. Simple. It's not about dominating. It's about reconnecting.

"Now that I'm a little more clear headed," I start, getting cut off by his laughing. I chuckle along with him, shaking my head and propping up on my elbow. "I can understand where you're coming from. You felt that connection. I'll give you the freedom to explore that, as long as you promise me that you'll be completely honest along the way?" That's all I'm asking of him. I just need to know where I stand with him.

"If I wanted to get rid of you, I could have easily poisoned you and made it look like a suicide," he teases, shoving away from me. With a playful growl, I yank him back to my body, biting down on his shoulder. "But I understand what you're saying. I've been gay for as long as I can remember. I hate keeping secrets, which you know as much as I do, that they're relationship killers. If anything, I may be tempted to offer her a piece of you too." He winks before jabbing me in the ribs with his elbow.

He rolls away quickly, standing before I can reach him and flopping face first into the sheets. I pout at him as he moves around the room, closing the windows and shutting off the lights. The fan is a must, so he flicks it on before returning to our designated spaces.

The large guy rolls right into my awaiting arms, taking his place as the little spoon.

Several moments go by, and my brain can't seem to shut off. "You promise you're not going to leave me?" With a dramatic sigh, he rolls over so we're face to face. Holding my jaw with his available arm, he levels our gazes.

"You ask me that again, and I will castrate you. I'm. Not. Leaving. You." He emphasizes every word to ensure that it'll penetrate my brain. Unfortunately, insecurity isn't cured with words.

We'll just have to wait and see.

Chapter Eight

Aspen

"**Y**ou're meant to be resilient, girl. No wonder daddy sold you off," Charles snickers, dancing the blade up my face. It's already dripping in blood. My blood. The edge is slightly dull, not enough to cut without firm pressure.

"Go to hell," I shriek. Cord wraps so tightly around my wrists that it's cutting off circulation. My legs splayed outward for easy access, where they want to be able to have me without the struggle.

The buyer returned me for having a 'filthy mouth'. Men are the bane of our existence. I've threatened my handler since I first came into captivity.

"We're already here, I guess I should have welcomed you." Ravi stands off to the side in the shadows, his hulking figure slumped into a chair as he jacks off to my struggling.

"I'll get out and kill you both," I hiss, spitting blood directly into his eyes. He doesn't stop. He presses down harder, still not breaking the skin of my face.

"If I wasn't preparing you for your next buyer, I'd have sliced this gorgeous face. Unfortunately, you've lost me quite a lot of money by *being a naughty girl. You do know what happens to bad girls, don't you?" His yellowed grin is almost so vile you can see the green poof. Tossing the knife, he brings the handle into my jaw.*

Thump.

What the fuck?

Looking around, the guys have vanished, leaving me strapped on the metal table.

Thump.

Thump.

"Wake up you stupid whore," Stephan spits, jabbing my side with a hot poker rod.

"You awake?" A soft voice asks. My eyes spring open, catching a woman with a clipboard. I attempt to scramble backward, only to have shooting pains in my entire body. A whimper floods from my mouth, tears leaking in my ducts.

I can't stay here. They'll find me.

Yanking on the cords, I can barely hear words being spewed at me. Hands grapple with mine as we fight. My mission is to take all of this off. They'll put me back under.

"It's okay," the woman shushes as I swat around myself. *No, it's not*, I want to scream. She doesn't know my pain, doesn't know my terror. She'll return me to them. Bounty money. Chest tightening, I finally rip the butterfly needle from my body.

"Code white, I repeat..." her voice slows as the world spins. There's suddenly multiple people pouring into the room as my eyes cross. I attempt to kick my legs over, only to be stopped by a metal railing.

"Please let me go," I whimper, watching as one guy in particular slowly walks up to me. He looks oddly familiar, the look on his face one I don't recognize. Dots dance in my vision as I try my hardest to focus. "Help me..."

"You can't handle a little blood loss?" Ravi laughs, whipping the bloody knife on his shirt. "You just had to bite me, didn't you? Couldn't do what you were told?"

"You know I never will!" Fighting against the bindings, another click on the cuffs resounds. Shit.

"All spirits are meant to be broken, darling girl." He comes closer, his pants only unbuttoned. "I can't talk about it." He says, suddenly stopping.

"What?" I retort, confusion lapping my brain.

"It's not my secret to share," he shrugs, backing away. Brows furrowing, I try to scream at him. Nothing comes out.

His figure suddenly vanishes into thin air, dust flying in the wind. I try to struggle, but it's as if my body is weighed down by a ton of bricks. Darkness envelops me as my brain goes light. Airy.

"How do you know her?" One guy barks quietly, obviously worked up. The tone he uses forces my body to relax, but I *need* to wake up. Sitting here while they argue only makes the chances of me being taken again higher. It's like I'm paralyzed. Almost like those dark dreams I used to have, ones where I'd stare into the darkness only to see people and monsters looking back at me. I'd never be able to do anything about them, even as they tormented me and ripped me apart.

"I think we should wait for her to wake up." Her voice...where do I know it from? Trying to pry my eyes open seems to be more of an effort than I remember. Light penetrates beneath my closed lids, lighting part of the darkness. I can see figures shadowing my bed, but they're not getting closer. They're simply there.

If I opened my eyes, would they be haunting me too?

Focusing my energy on moving, it feels as though there's white static stuck in my body. My limbs are sleeping, failing to wake up even when danger is present.

I have to get out of here! I scream internally, shifting my eyes to the shadows. They move, their chatter falling silent as my heart hammers in my chest. I try even harder to do something. *Anything.* Breathing seems impossible as they move around me, their tones escalating. What they're saying is damn near irrelevant. I have to get out of here.

Let me go!

"Guys," a gruff voice calls quietly, but the others talk over him. The muffled sounds make it hard to distinguish what they're saying. Chair screeching and a harsh clattering, my body finally gives a response. They slam open on their own, ignoring the harsh fluorescents as I look around. Two large guys and two females are staring at me, presumably in shock.

If anything, I probably have the same expression as they do. Except, I'm the first to react. Swinging my good leg over the side, I quickly grapple with the wires again. Once I'm free, I can work with the solid weight on my other one. Pain grips me, but it stopped me last time. It won't stop me again.

They're all here for me, and I know that one against four odds aren't great, but if I move fast enough-

"That's enough," he barks, stomping over to me and ripping my hands away from my arms. In swift succession, he rolls me back onto the bed with my arms high above my head. It didn't take any effort on his part to get me to stop. In my moment of surprise, I stop to take a good look at the guy. His dark beard is heavy and thick, definitely untamed like his long hair. He's got tattoos leading all over his body. Just like...

"Get off me," I snarl, trying to buck my hips.

"Listen here, little lady," he retorts, pointing a finger on his free hand. "You just endured a fucking surgery that required plates and shit to repair your leg. We didn't kidnap you, in fact, they've done everything they could to save you. How about a little gratitude?" Staring at him in shock, my body won't respond with anything other than my jaw dropping open. With an eye roll, he pushes away from me.

"I'm Doctor Solla," a female says, tugging the man back gently. "That's Nomad, over there is Techy, and that is Heallie." She points to another guy and a female with bright blue scrubs on. Heallie pops a bubble before pulling her hair back into a ponytail.

I attempt to say something, but all that comes out is air. Swallowing even seems to be a challenge. My heart hammers against my sternum as I try to calm myself down.

They're not trying to help you. In it for themselves!

"Your vocals are strained from the struggle as well as malnourishment. We've got you on antibiotics and pain relievers. As Mr. Gruff over there mentioned, we had to conduct an extensive surgery on your leg. If you've not even noticed yet, you have an external fixator on your leg." Looking down, I realize I've got a giant metal bracket around my leg with pins disappearing into it.

"A what?" I rasp, knocking my fist against my chest to get more air.

"An external fixator. Basically, it fixes your bone from the outside. Due to the severity, we placed several rods and plates in your bone. The fixator helps keep the bone in place from the outside. Pins are attached then routed to the bars here." She points to a few of them on the inside. "It just holds your bones together while they heal."

"Why not just use a cast?" I retort, slapping a hand to my mouth quickly. "I'm sorry, I didn't mean that-"

"Don't worry," she urges, a non-predatory smile on her face. "A cast really doesn't do the same thing that a fixator does. Due to the severity, you will need another surgery. For now, it helps with getting you back on your feet with a form of stability until your overall health is better. I would go over why other forms of treatment were inappropriate, but then I'd be overloading you with medical terminology mumbo-jumbo."

Words can't compute inside my brain, so I simply nod. What more could I say? She's right, I'm already overstimulated with information.

Looking back down at the bracket thing on my leg, it's at least silver, not black or gold.

"Are you allergic to anything, Aspen?" Dr. Solla asks, flipping through her chart.

"Uhm, penicillin...I didn't give you my name," I pause, my calming heart rate jumping back up. Blood rushes to my head as I focus on the brace.

This was a ploy, you're not safe!

"You don't remember me?" She asks softly, leaning down to meet my eyes.

I stare at her for what seems like hours, trying to formulate thoughts. Sadly, I can't seem to remember much of my old life. Only the new memories and the people who dumped me for money.

"No," I whisper, shifting them to look elsewhere, only to grab the attention of the gruff male. Arms crossed over his chest, his fists are clenched tightly beneath his biceps. Another guy, a little shorter than his counterpart, stands with his hand resting over the bearded guys. Switching between the two, I can sense something between them.

"Is that normal?" Short one whispers, catching the attention of Dr. Solla. She nods, writing stuff on her notepad. Another fuck expression I can't read.

You've been isolated. They've trained you.

"We better give you some time to rest," she suggests, standing from the rolling chair. "Just know, there's a guard at the door and the window is locked. This is simply for your protection. I'd like to keep you overnight, then you're free to roam with these two." She points at gruff and gruffer with a smile.

With no clock in sight, I can't even try to create a sense of time. Something I lacked prior to this bullshit.

"How long have I been out?" I mutter, pulling the sheets over my exposed lower half. Bruises that I didn't realize were on display are now covered. The tattoo I forgot about pulses on my thigh like a second heartbeat. Probably from infection.

"Techy found you about a week ago," the gruff guy, Nomad, replies softly. He looks to his counterpart with tender eyes, kissing his forehead lovingly. My throat grows tight at the sight, tears threatening to overtake me.

"A week?" I hoarsely whisper around the lump sitting in my airway. "Has anyone..." I can't even finish the sentence.

"No," Nomad barks, taking a step forward then stopping. He huffs out, sliding a large hand through the unruly hair. "We can talk about it once you're better."

With that, he turns on his heel leaving the room like it's on fire.

Chapter Nine

Aspen

"How are you feeling today?" Dr. Solla asks, sitting on the stool and gliding right up to me.

"Physically?" I ask, turning my head to look at her. She's got my upper body propped up slightly and my leg hanging from this ceiling contraption thing. It's like a sling, except it's not. Even the slight movement of my head makes my body feel ten times its normal weight.

"Whatever your interpretation of the question is," she returns, leveling me.

Overnight was fucking awful. After finding out that I was in a sort of medical induced coma, it's been a rollercoaster of pain and emotions. At some point in the middle of the night, there were ghosts taunting me and warning me about the bounty laid out for me. I may or may not have panicked enough to get a shot of some good shit.

Okay, it wasn't good shit, but it took the mean people away. That's all I truly care about.

Besides the mental turmoil my brain decided I needed to endure, it also put my body through the ringer.

"I feel like a mac truck ran over me, realized it only got my upper half, then backed up over my legs and went forward again over my leg." She chokes back a laugh before turning to the paper chart.

"I'll write down that you're in pain," she quips, flicking her eyes up to me for a moment. "Do you know when your pain starts? How long between medication rounds?"

"I'm not sure. I didn't think to time it between all my loony episodes." She releases a heavy sigh, placing the documents on her lap and lacing her fingers.

"Look, Aspen. I know this isn't ideal. You're safe here with the guys. Yes, I'm new to the club. My husband was recently patched in, and I knew I could be of service to them. The things they do to protect their own," she pauses, a look of longing on her face.

"But that's the thing," I interrupt before she can continue. "I'm not one of them. I don't have anything to offer to the club. Shit, if it makes matters worse, I can't even be in a room with a guy without feeling as if I'm going to pass out. You're grouping me with people who are at least semi-normal. Just let me go, and I'll figure it out."

She doesn't say anything for a long moment, staring at me with a look I can't quite decipher. Narrowing her eyes, she nods.

"Then let's talk about it," she says, leaning back against the wall. "You don't associate yourself with 'normal'. Let's unpack that a bit."

Without thinking, I laugh.

It's like a reflex I can't stop now that it's started.

"You think," I pause, catching my breath, "that talking about it is going to make it go away?"

"Isn't that how a lot of people overcome trauma? There's also exposure therapy," she points out, crossing her legs over one another, fingers crossing again.

"You think talking about it is going to magically make me be able to be in the same room as another guy? Let alone multiple?" I retort, irritation festering in my chest. She's not getting what I'm saying. The shit I went through...the only reason I'm not shitting bricks is because she's not threatening.

You can never be too certain...maybe she's here just for you.

"Is that what I said?" She quips, tilting a brow at me. "I'm not asking you to overcome your biggest fear within a conversation. Hell, Aspen, I'm not even asking you to talk about your fears right now. We'd love to be able to help you. I only know your name because..." she trails off, looking down for a moment.

"Because what?" I press, scooting up the bed a bit.

"It's not relevant. The club is ready and willing to support you whether you're an ol' lady or not. Your brain won't let you get over that fear, fine. That's a long term goal." She clicks her pen and writes down little scribbles. I look like a damn fish with my mouth opening and closing. Words just don't seem to formulate.

"You don't get to move on from a subject that you think is irrelevant," I snap, fisting one hand in the sheets. The dam's . "I have no fucking clue who you are, yet you know my first name? Do you know anything else about me? Birthday? Social security number?"

"You're making this a bigger deal than it needs to be," she sighs, pinching the bridge of her nose. "If it makes you feel better, no, I don't know any of that. I know your name because-"

"Enough," a deep voice growls. As if on instinct, my jaw snaps shut. Narrowing my eyes, Nomad saunters into the room. Again, the fear ramps in my chest tenfold.

Except, it's not the terror I'm used to feeling. This is a different type of fear, one that is completely foreign to me. One that has my heart pumping in my chest, stomach fluttering, yet I can't look at a dude's dick without wanting to vomit.

Just ask Ravi.

He's gruff and aggressive, voice rough as nails on a chalkboard. Yet, I can't help the slight flutter my lower lady parts get when seeing his raggedness.

You're attracted to the demon specimen that hurt you.

Tortured you.

Shaking my head, I keep my eyes lowered to his chest. Looking at him directly could initiate a challenge. That's a mistake you'll only ever make once.

"Nomad," she nods, standing from her seat. Their hands meet in a slight shake before she sits back down. He takes the hard plastic chair next to my bed and propping himself on his elbows. I scoot as far away from him as I possibly can without falling off the bed. Swallowing thickly, I flicker between the two. They're having a silent conversation with brows raising before they both turn to me.

No good things come from those types of conversations.

"I'd like a minute alone with you." He turns to look at me after a while, and I can't help retreating. My eyes shift to the sheets. When he reaches for me, the involuntary flinch only makes the silence thicker.

"No, thank you," I whisper, trailing over my propped leg. It still gives me the chills seeing several metal pieces sticking into my skin. Shaving that is going to be a bitch.

They'll probably just wax it, like the others.

"Would you feel more comfortable with my counterpart?" He responds surprisingly softly, nodding toward the door. If I remember correctly, Techy is his husband. "Techy is my husband, yes," he affirms my silent, or I guess not so silent, question.

You don't really get an option.

I clasp my hands together tightly with a shrug, acting as nonchalantly as I can with two giant men in the room. With my five foot two frame, they're like monsters. There's a slight tremble in my hands that I work to contain.

"These aren't ideal circumstances, I know, but we're really only here to help you," Techy rasps, taking Dr. Solla's place as she makes her way out.

"I'll come back in a little while to check on you. I'll send Heallie to bring that medication." With that, she shuts the door behind her softly.

You're cornered, just how you like it.

"Whatever you need, you can have," Nomad comments, keeping his gaze directed to me. "Do you have family or friends that we can reach out to?"

"No!" I bark quickly, slapping a hand over my mouth. The movement jostles my leg and sends a rocket of pain through my body. Breathe through it.

Just like all the other times. Breathe through it.

Real terror seeps into my veins, when everything suddenly starts moving all at once. There's suddenly two of him and two of Nomad. My stomach rolls as the terror mixes with the lightning pain.

"Woah, easy," Techy gasps, reaching forward. I jolt to get away from him, but in my haste, the lines attached to my arm force the metal IV stand to tip towards me. Before I can think, I grab it and move it out of my way.

Chapter Ten

NOMAD

"**S**hit!" Techy shouts, flying out of his chair and ducking down. A stand flies toward him at an alarming rate, clattering against the wall and embedding slightly. Shock ripples through me as the tiny girl struggles against everything around her.

She's in a state I used to see quite often.

Fight or flight.

"Hey, hey," I call, keeping my hands poised up and in surrender. Her body is partially on the bed, her braced leg barely on it. We didn't get specifics if she could bear weight on it or not, but I'd rather not find out the hard way.

"Get away from me!" She screams, the look in her eyes is one that's almost crazed. As if she's not actually here. Maybe her brain transported her out of herself in an effort to protect her...

What has she gone through?

Taking a step forward, I slowly inch my hands out to her. Without warning, her eyes cross, her good leg gives out, and her whole body tumbles to the ground. Metal on the fixator thing scrapes on the ground.

Techy and I both curse, launching to help her. Her head cracks on the stone flooring, bouncing harshly while the rest of her limbs flail. A pitiful whimper pushes from between her lips. The blood pumping organ in my chest batters against its confines.

Pure, unadulterated horror echoes from my brain as I move cautiously toward the spooked girl. The last thing I want is for her to wake up and see me then start her rampage all over again.

Techy helps me gather the small girl, and together, we gently lift her back to the slight indent where she'd been resting. Her hair is thick on her head, a tangled mess, but I'm able to weave through it enough to rule out any lacerations. My husband repositions her leg before pressing the call button for either Heallie or Doc.

"What the actual fuck was that?" He mutters, slumping heavily into the chair. Before I can open my mouth, Heallie waltzes in with a small cup in her hand and the paper chart.

"Oh, she fell asleep!" She deduces brightly, setting the chart at the foot of the bed.

"Actually, not quite," I sigh, rubbing the tension out of the back of my neck. Between Techy and I, we silently decide that I'll be the one to tell the tale. "I'm not really sure what spurred it on, to be frank. We were telling her about her place here then she moves, her lines were pulled, we reached for her because she was about to fucking rip them out." Shoving my fingers through my hair, I softly tug them.

"So, that would explain the IV pole sticking out of the wall," she hums, thumbing over her shoulder. "Doc was saying that the girl has gone through some pretty tough shit." Heallie moves around the room, opening cabinets and punching in codes before putting a syringe into the main line.

"What's that?" I ask, but it comes out more of a demand. She quirks a brow at me, before twisting it and showing me the label. *Saline solution.*

"Either way, Aspen has been a true trooper for her circumstances. I don't know the details, but I know the look. I've only ever witnessed those exact symptoms when I was working in the trafficking unit before I met my man." Pushing the solution into the line, she nods for Techy to hold the bag for her while she retrieves the stand.

"That's what we gathered." She gets the lines all put back into place, readjusts Aspen's stuff before nodding.

"I'll be back to warn her of moving. I swear, I'd strap her down if I knew it wouldn't cause a big fight." Shaking her head, she writes notes on the chart before heading toward the door.

"Heallie," Techy calls, a look of curiosity on his features. I've seen that look before. It's one that may or may not get him into trouble later. "How would we be able to pull her out of this...funk?" She laughs, leaning against the wall.

"Well, therapy is a great start," she points out, looking at the sleeping girl. "Honestly? I think you know someone else who has the answer to that question." With that, she turns on her clog covered heel and shuts the door behind her.

"I can't believe what you're suggesting," I scoff, disappointment unfurling in my stomach. "For the most obvious reasons, that wouldn't work."

"Babe, how do you know that?" He argues, leaning his elbows on his knees. "Just ask Widower! She underwent traumatic shit and was able to come out on the other side!"

"Pax, she wasn't riddled with trauma based around sex," I remind him gently, just in case the girl roused. "Take into consideration the fact that she was held captive. What if whips and chains are a trigger for her?"

"How do you know they aren't?" He asks, the same sassy ass male who grates my nerves.

"I'm about to tan your ass," I grunt, clenching my fists and forcing myself to stay seated. "You're not understanding this, baby. She lacked that control."

"Right," he agrees, looking at me as if I'm on the same page as him. "Think about it. She could take back that control if she wanted. It may be different, sure, but it would give her that empowerment."

"You're also talking about a girl who can't even be around men. Skittish if they move too quickly around her."

"Okay then we use another female," he retorts, like it's the most common thing in the world. Unfortunately, he's only seen the good side of BDSM. He may have had to join the club for less than great circumstances, but he's not had to endure a bad dominant.

I've had to endure his sassy submission though. Fucking brat.

"Do you think she'll want to control another female, knowing what it's like to be controlled?" I ask, which finally seems to make him go silent. "You've not seen how bad the world can be because I've done my job as your husband in protecting you. If I could forever avoid you seeing or even hearing about it, I would. This girl has fallen into our laps, and you said it yourself that you're attached. Is that still the case?"

His eyes shift from me to the gorgeous girl laying in the bed. Pale complexion, eyes and cheeks sunken, I can still see the beauty that she is. That damn blood pumping organ starts hammering faster at the thought of her being abused.

She's got patches of hair missing, scars and bruises marring her body. I'll be one to admit that those permanent marks only make someone that much hotter, but these aren't self-inflicted or good story scars. The story is sinister, one that will most likely never be shared with the next generation.

"Absolutely," he says with finality. Hesitantly, he reaches for her hand and cups it in his.

"It won't be easy," I note, giving him one last chance to bow out. Even I'm growing attached to the small female.

"I know, but she'll be amazing one day, and that's what I'm looking forward to."

I just hope he's right.

Chapter Eleven

ONE MONTH LATER

 TECHY

"I still don't think it's a good idea," Widower says, taking a sip of her virgin drink. Her face skews slightly, which I'm assuming is because it lacks the good shit.

"You and Nomad talked, huh?" I huff, crossing my arms over my chest. Leaning back in the barstool, I twist around and look out at the club.

"I mean, he's my vice, so I kind of have to." She turns toward me, leaning an elbow on the bartop. "Look, the intentions are good. She's made exceptional progress, give credit where it's due, but you're suggesting a type of exposure therapy."

Some of the guys stand around as a sort of protection shield while Aspen talks with Maggie, helping with the kids. Over the last month, the club has shown a level of compassion that I didn't think they contained. While they've kept their distance, they also work to fend off any outsiders who come just to hang out from approaching her.

Nomad and I have also worked really hard in getting her to open up to us. She's not said anything about what led to this shit, but she doesn't jump with quick movements around the guys anymore. The female prospects have been amazing about making her feel more comfortable. Even now, they've got her leg propped on the cushion of the booth, making sure the metal doesn't catch.

"I think BDSM would be perfect for her," I mutter, spinning back and downing the rest of my drink. "We just need to know her triggers."

Widower scoffs, shaking her head. "Has she told you anything about what makes her tick?"

"Well, no," I start, looking into my cup.

"Let's be real here, Techy. She's not the kind of girl you're going to get into bed with quickly," she says, rapping a knuckle on the top. "She's got clothes covering all over her body except the frame on her leg. Have you spoken to Doc?"

Sighing, I hold my glass up for a refill. "No, I haven't. Doc won't talk without Aspen's consent."

"We really need to get her a new name," Widower huffs, eyes the girl over her shoulder. "I'll chat with Doc, see what I can find out. You need to work on *slowly* adjusting her lifestyle."

"Nomad and I are trying," I retort, irritation spiking in my stomach. "It's been difficult trying to juggle work, the prospects, my own marriage, and her. The thing is, I can't just let her go. There's this...pull that I have toward her. Nomad feels it, and we're working her out of her comfort zone every day."

"You're nervous that she won't be into it," she states, nodding along.

"I mean, that's one obvious question. Another one would be if she's actually interested in men at all, at this point." My heart hammers at the possibility that she's not even interested. Not that I'd blame her. Men are garbage unless you find the right one.

Thinking back to how much growth she's had in just this month, it's hard not to think that this could be real. I swear we flirt back and forth, yet that could very well just be her personality. During the days she's stuck at the club with me, she expresses interest in learning about different systems, how they run, how we track people for the executioners or runners.

"Why don't you just talk to her?" Widower finally asks, pushing the empty glass away from her and standing. "For all you know, she's just waiting to get the hell out of dodge." With that, she turns on her heel and heads in the direction of the office. Hudson meets her halfway, sliding into the room. Chuckling, I stand up and stretch a bit, debating my next moves.

Widower's right about the name thing, though. We can't officially assign her a road name without her joining the club. She's not expressed an interest, but she's really close with Maggie and the female prospects. Dropping a few bills on the counter top, I stroll to where they're sitting. Aspen talks animatedly with Maggie about motorcycles, how Maggie is helping her husband Crusher with modifying his hell rider. He's trying to make it go a hell of a lot faster.

"Ladies," I smirk, locking eyes with Aspen and leaning on the back of the chair. "This seat taken?"

"Join us," she smiles, waving freely. The difference I've seen in her, how her cheeks aren't as shallow nor her eyes gaunty. It's a great change, that's for damn sure.

"He talked about painting it pussy pink," Maggie scoffs, clinking the ice in her glass. "I was trying to figure out what exactly that color was, so he bent me over the bike and railed me into the next day!" The other girls laugh while Aspen simply smiles, but it's better than the cringing.

"Girl, you've gotten more adventurous since the twins!" Stella, one of the prospects giggles, sloshing back her drink. I've seen her around before, she's one of Crusher's prospects. Once he stepped back from Vice for Nomad, he decided he'd start doing training.

"You've got no idea," Maggie sighs, a dazed look in her eyes.

"Techy, escape while you can," Aspen softly calls, giggling into her hand. Maggie goes to swat her on the arm. Aspen doesn't flinch, but she tenses up, her back pin straight.

"Shit, I'm sorry!" Maggie gasps, putting her hands under her bottom. "I always forget-"

"It's fine," Aspen reassures, smiling softly and placing a tentative hand on her shoulder. "Did you come over for something, Techy?" The look on her face says it all.

"Actually, I need to speak with you in private," I hint. She damn near jumps to stand up and get out of her seat. The girls jump with her, trying to move out of her way without snagging her fixator on anything.

"Thank you for sitting with me," she says politely, turning to smile at the girls. They all say their goodbyes before Aspen practically runs away. Due to the thing on her leg, she can't move faster than a limp walk, but I digress.

"I was starting to get tired," she laughs, her voice soft as always. "These medications don't give the exhaustion side effect enough credit."

"Is that normal?" I open the door to my office, waiting while she gathers her courage to enter it. To both of our surprise, Nomad is already sitting there.

Naked.

"Oh shit!" He curses while she squeals, and he jumps up to grab the blanket from over the couch. "Shit, I didn't think," he sputters. His cock tries to poke through the material of the blanket, still obviously hard from before.

"It's fine," she squeaks, her hands balled into fists at her sides. I'd expected her to have covered her eyes with them. But instead, she trails her eyes over his naked form. I can see the shiver go down his spine from here, his thick cock jumping behind the blanket.

"Let me just..." he turns on his heel, storming to the bathroom. His ass jiggles as he walks, and I can't help the laugh that escapes me. This definitely isn't what I expected.

"Well, what a way to start a meeting!" Motioning her further into the room, I shut the door behind me and take a seat at the desk. Her eyes are still cast to where Nomad took off to, her face one of longing.

"You okay?" I ask, my stomach churning slightly. I don't want this to put her off. We've worked so hard to ensure that she's safe and comfortable around us. She hasn't been around very long, too short to say whether we're making a ton of progress to getting her hold back to her old self or not.

I just hope this didn't sway her away from everything.

Chapter Twelve

I want more.

It's weird to think because the one thing I'd promised myself was that I'd never get involved with men. They're vile creatures who are a bane to female existence. Then, I'm practically abducted by Satan's Wheels MC and given food and shelter. Different guys from nowhere bring me things that help my recovery like blankets, soaps, and other girly shit that I need. Maybe the females put them up to it, possibly could be them thinking I'm just a shiny new toy. Yet, they don't treat me like one. In a sense, they're almost too scared to approach me.

However, when I saw Nomad sitting there, stroking himself, my legs shook slightly. The sexualism I thought I lost is racing back into my body as if it never went away. Unfortunately, I know that I'm not into women. I've tried the past couple weeks to just be interested sexually, but it's just not there. That or no one has caught my fancy. Either way, it's not happening. Meeting with Doc nearly everyday was hard to cope with at first, but her and these two guys have been nothing if not supportive.

They weren't kidding when they said they'd be there for me.

It was just a sneak peak at his bare manhood, the thick veins swirling down his cock that were almost taunting me.

Am I really fucking crazy?

I just escaped captivity. Ran for my fucking life, and here I am, practically throwing myself onto his cock.

Maybe that's why daddy sold you. You're a whore.

Shaking my head, I loosen my fists. A tickle on the inside of my palm catches my attention. Looking down, I realize I've drawn blood.

"Shit, sit down," Techy says, moving quickly around the room. I steady my breathing and force my anxiously racing heart to slow.

You're a freak. Sell yourself back, they'll satisfy you.

Squeezing my eyes closed, I dig the palm of my hands into the sockets. The sting from oncoming tears burns behind my lids. I do everything in power to hold the sob in.

"Fuck, I didn't know you were going to be here," Nomad grunts, plopping down next to me and placing a gentle hand on my back. Rough jean material rubs against my leggings, the warmth radiating from his body. He rubs soothing circles while my throat constricts, finally forcing me to release the pent up sounds. It's stupid because I should be scared shitless, running for my life. Yet, I'm sitting here, pretending that all is well and my life isn't a waste of air.

"It's not you," I sob, scrubbing my hands up and into my hair. The roots are tugged tightly as I fight the silent voices in my head, the images of everything I went through flashing before me. It's like I can still feel their hands grabbing at me, pushing me around, pulling at my skin.

"Do you want me to call Doc?" Techy asks, pushing my hair away from my face. Shaking my head, it all falls back to where it was. Again, he moves it.

"Tell me what I can do to fix this," Nomad rasps, almost like a plea. A mirthless laugh boils over, the sound mixed with the sob.

"I'm the one that's fucked up." Turning, I feel the tears streaming down my face change angle. He raises his hand, and I nod, the silent permission for him to touch me. A gentle finger drags over my cheek before pulling back. I didn't care about the blood, lest forgetting about it completely.

"I'm not sure what's going through that pretty head of yours. It may have been a surprise, sure. Crashing into our lives hasn't been easy for any of us, but I will continue to tell you that you're worth pursuing." Nomad brings the finger of blood to his mouth, sucking it in and licking it clean. I don't know whether to be disgusted or turned on.

Definitely both.

Without thinking, I practically throw myself at Nomad, slanting his lips over mine. His hands automatically clasp on my hips to keep me from moving, a comfortable heat radiating from him.

Is this a shitty time to admit that I've never kissed anyone before?

Neither of us move. My eyes slammed shut when I pounced, so I have no idea if his are open or what Techy is thinking.

Shit. You just assaulted his husband.

Jerking back quickly, I realize I didn't ask for permission. If someone did that to me, I'd have screamed bloody murder. I shove myself off of him, limping slightly at the impact on my leg. A sharp zing levels through it, but it doesn't stop me from backing up until

I bump into the wall. Neither guy moves. Nomad's eyes are closed, hands fisted next to him while Techy just looks stunned.

"I'm sorry," I rasp, my mental barriers slowly pushing themselves back into place.

You practically raped him, stupid girl.

Just like they did to you, you did to him.

"Woah, Aspen," Techy starts, bringing his hands up in surrender. "No one is mad at you. We're all just surprised." He stands, cautiously walking toward me. The metal on my fixator bumps the wall, the clang signaling that I'm not going anywhere.

"I didn't...he didn't..." I can't form any words to try and explain myself. Running my hands through my hair, I force myself to relax.

Neither of them are mad at me. If they were, they'd have dragged me down to their imprisonment and tortured me. Right?

Using that mentality, I continue to work myself into relaxing. In theory, if they were going to hurt me, they already would have.

"Can I?" Nomad asks, standing closer to me than I remember. He must have made his way over while I was working myself out of loony-ville. His arms are outstretched. I don't hesitate. Nodding, he scoops me up in his arms and gently wraps me around his large body. Techy takes up the rear, laying his head on my shoulder as I snuggle into Nomad's chest.

His pinewood smell mixes with something else, like a manly musk I can't really identify.

I'm being carried back over to the offending couch and plopped onto Nomad's lap with Techy right there with us.

"I'd brought you up here to go over club stuff," Techy mumbles into my clothes, nuzzling my neck. The stubble tickles my sensitive skin, forcing me to laugh at the feeling. Both men tense up, before

I realize that I'm practically grinding my crotch onto Nomad's. Stopping instantly, I nibble on my bottom lip while avoiding eye contact with either of them.

I can't think about sex without having nightmares, so why is it that I want to jump both of their fucking bones.

Whores can't have their cake and eat it too.

Rolling my eyes at the bitch in my head, I contain my initial urge to get down. Something I've learned about the two guys in the past month, is that if they want something, they'll say it. The fact that Nomad hasn't forced me onto my feet stops me from wriggling out of his arms.

"We wanted to talk about making you an official member of the club, even if you're not fully patched in. Kind of like Maggie." I swear my heart stops. That would mean stability.

Would I be able to leave when I want? Could I run if *they* found me?

"I don't know what goes on in that beautiful head of yours, but I want to continue to tell you that you have no need to be scared of us." Techy's words heat my skin and sink into my body. My brain rejects them, but my heart...it takes them, twists them, and forces them into my veins. It wants to be happy. My entire being is more than ready for a little bit of happiness.

My mouth opens to respond, but nothing escapes. Not even air.

"Maybe when you're able to buy yourself back you can have some freedom," Ravi's voice echoes in my head.

"Fuck off," I snap, burrowing my head further into his chest. Nomad leans away while Techy tilts my head up. Both men stare at me with worry.

"Do I need to call Doc?" Techy asks again, leveling me with a single look. My throat constricts as I try to figure out what I'm doing. I've never been able to iron down what I want to do, but being here with these two? It's like everything is falling into place.

It's almost too damn perfect.

"No," I mutter, flicking between the two men. There's a passive curiosity on Techy's face while Nomad looks about ready to take me to Doc himself. "I promise I'm fine. It's just..." I pause.

"You don't have to talk if you don't want to," Nomad reassures, pressing his warm lips to my forehead.

"You're more than welcome to say no to the offer." Techy brushes his fingers over my spine, massaging as he goes. "It's a better way to conceal your identity. We'll have to gather information for paperwork, but we'd prefer to give you an alias than to use your name. I'm not sure how common Aspen is, but we wanted to give you something cool. Something that represents who you are and how you're progressing. We need to work on concealing who you are and rebranding you. Your health comes first above all else, but your safety is right up there with it. You don't have to talk about it now, just consider it."

In all honesty, I want to be able to talk about it. They say that shit is better out in the open than bottled up. I just don't know if I can do it without breaking down. Doc worked with me several times to bring me back from the point of no return, if my drift is caught. What if I say something then end up pushing myself past that point? I don't *want* to die, but I'd rather that over the constant pain and suffering that this life has brought me.

"I don't know who did this to you or what circumstances lead to this, but we're working so fucking hard to make sure you can have your revenge. When we find out who..." his baritone voice is almost like a lullaby, if I wasn't being pressed into an erection that is barely contained by jeans.

"Please don't," I whisper, feeling the tears leaking from my eyes once more. Containing them is near impossible, but I figure it's easier to let them fall where I won't be judged.

"We just want you to know that we'll cut off their cocks and shove them down their own throats for you," Techy states determinedly, his brows scrunching downward. I can't help the laugh that escapes me from his seriousness. I'd love nothing more than to get my revenge, but the way he said it.

Maybe I'm going crazy. That definitely has to be it.

"I know," I whisper, taking several deep breaths. "I just want it all to go away."

"It won't go away," Nomad mutters, nuzzling his head on mine. "You'll just get a hell of a lot stronger."

"What about exposure therapy?" Techy asks, brushing his fingers through my hair.

Chapter Thirteen

Aspen

T his wasn't what I had in mind when he mentioned exposure therapy.

When Techy talked about it a few nights ago, I didn't think he meant me actually going back to a ball and chain. Apparently, that's exactly what he meant. Well, at least a version of it.

Walking down the stairs, I can hear the soft music strumming, the bass hitting the speakers heavily. It's only ten in the morning, but the two men decided that it would be best to start with an empty club instead of diving right into scenes. If I didn't know any better, I would have anticipated people gyrating on one another, practically screwing on the dancefloor. To say I'm thankful it's empty...

Finally landing on the bottom stair, my heart beats quickly from the exertion of the trek. Since being here, I've eaten better than I have my entire life, but solid foods are still a bitch to keep down. So, physical exercise has taken the back burner in most cases. Stairs are the necessary evil to get down to the club, so I've endured it with little complaint.

I've also made it extremely clear that I'm open to getting back on the right track. No one wants to be crippled by crushing anxiety, but here I am. The walking, talking version. If you opened the dictionary to the word 'anxiety' my face would be the first thing you see.

The pressure in my chest only increases as I look at the walls seeing sensual photos of men and women bound and strung around. My mouth is catching flies at this point because I'm both intrigued and appalled.

Rounding on the two men, I don't even know what to say. "I wasn't expecting this," I go with instead. They both laugh. I'm way out of my comfort level here.

"You're not going to do that anytime soon," Nomad reassures gently, his deep voice slightly raspy with the work to remain quiet. A ball weighs heavily in my throat, and it stays unmoving as I attempt to swallow it down. No matter the amount of comfort, I'd much rather just not be here. Seeing this shit...

"You just love to be tied, don't you?" Charles coos, dragging the knife down my face. Stephan steps up next to him, testing the boundaries of my restraints. I remain motionless. Consequences to moving tend to be worse than just enduring what they give me.

"Answer me!" He snaps, grabbing my throat and cutting off air. The knife digs further into my cheek, and I try to rasp out an answer. Nothing will come out, but I nod to appease him.

He seems to take that answer, letting go of my neck and stepping back. Cool liquid trickles down my face, the sting from the blade as it tears through my skin.

"Look at these tits," Stephan barks, laughing loudly. He digs the tip of the knife into my breast, bouncing it while it threatens to impale

me. Sobs escape me as the point sinks into the underside, before he pushes it back off.

"I think she's ready for more, don't you think?" Ravi questions, digging his nails into my skin as he walks around my body.

"Please, don't," I whimper, accidentally throwing in my displeasure. That's what gets you in trouble.

"Hey!"

Ravi snarls, pulling back and slamming his fist into my stomach. I attempt to curl into myself, but the restraints on my body stop me. My face grows red hot as I hold back the agony. They hate sounds of pain, even if they can't really distinguish my cries while they hurt me. While they do unspeakable things to me.

"You're going to beg me for it," Charles demands, stroking himself through his pants.

"Aspen!"

"Please," I beg, silently adding stop. *They laugh, surrounding me with ropes, whips, and knives.*

A hand smacks my face roughly, and I sputter, looking at the ceiling around me. Two hulking guys are hovering over me, both of their features are scrunched with concern.

"What..." Pausing, my head pounds harshly, my eyes have their own heartbeat.

"We're so fucking sorry," Techy sniffles, wiping at his eyes. "I didn't know or else I'd never-"

"It's fine," I scold, stopping him from going too far. It's not fucking fine that I apparently passed out. I wouldn't be staring at the ceiling if I didn't collapse.

"I called Doc, she's on her way." Techy looks seconds away from sobbing. Reaching up, I cup his cheek lightly. "You were right, it was too much too soon." He glances over at Nomad, sadness enveloping his features.

Blood rushes to my head as I try to sit up. Nomad pulls me toward him, putting my back to his chest and caging me in while Techy props my feet on his lap. The pressure in my brain hasn't subsided and I've not acquired the overwhelming urge to vomit. Doc's done everything she can to help sway the nightmares and day-mares away without using medications.

"What happened?" Doc barks, hustling toward us. Techy looks embarrassed while Nomad just looks indifferent.

"I wanted to try exposure therapy," I pipe up, deciding to take the blame. Both men swivel their heads to look at me, and I shake mine. "It's hard to constantly feel like I'm not good enough. I thought..."

"If you could get over it, you'd be fine," Doc huffs, frustration clear in her tone. "That's not how it works, Aspen." She kneels next to me, adjusting my left leg and looking at the fixator.

"We caught her before she could fall or hurt it," Techy says, rubbing his hands on my arms.

"For what it's worth, your progress is a lot faster than other survivors I've dealt with."

Scrunching up my face, I voice my distaste. "Please don't call me a survivor. It's not something I'm going to get through, and it's a label I'd like to avoid."

"But you are one," Techy quips, lacing his fingers with mine. "You're actively going through it and surviving day by day."

"Don't label me," I snap. Taking a clarifying breath like Doc taught me, I center myself. "It's like saying a woman is hot. We're not a temperature. I'm not a survivor. We all exist with demons, everyone is a survivor."

"Okay." Doc puts a stop to everything else. "Let's get you back to the clinic. I'd love to have you journal what you remember."

Even with my continued protests, the guys hoist me up and onto my feet, making sure I stay steady. Looping my arm through Doc's she guides me out of the club while yelling at the guys to give us some time.

The guys speak quietly, and as we take the steps one at a time, their voices fade until I can only hear my own labored breathing.

After several spotty points of thinking I'm going to pass out, we finally make it to the clinic. She helps me prop on the table and gets my leg situated in the sling thing. It's a stupid contraption, but the biggest priority is making sure I didn't hurt it.

She tells me to hang out for a few minutes as she leaves to go grab something. I stare at the tiles on the ceiling, counting them, losing track, then starting again. I recount to thirty before I wonder if I've double counted before starting over. After I've counted to thirty about ten times, I decide I'm done waiting.

That's when *he* walks in. And I swear I need the world to swallow me whole.

"No..."

Chapter Fourteen

TECHY

She walks away with Doc, and my heart rips out of my chest. The hurt and pain that I caused her...I didn't think this through. *Fuck*.

"Hey," Nomad says, throwing his arm over my shoulder. He brings me into his chest, and I can't help but inhale his musky scent. The pinewood is all-consuming as I let the tears finally fall. I'm not a little bitch by any means. I feel like a fucking prick for doing that to her.

"I'm such an idiot," I cry, wrapping my arms around his waist.

"It's not totally your fault. If she didn't want to come down here, she wouldn't have. Don't take the blame for something that was an accident. We all wanted this for her, including her." He shushes me and keeps me confined to his chest.

His fingers pinch my chin and force me to look up at him. Strong features look back at me, his eyes stern as he passes between my two.

"You know better," he mutters, pressing his lips to mine. Taking his time, he licks my bottom lip and pushes his tongue inside. His cock is already hard as he grinds against me, rubbing himself over my growing erection. "I want you to take back everything you said."

"No," I retort, pushing into him. He rears back, brows furrowing downward.

"What did you just say to me?" He growls, hand wrapping around my throat. I gasp, my semi-hard cock immediately stiffening as he manhandles me.

"I said..." I pause, lifting my chin in defiance. "No." A slow smile peels onto his face, head shaking while he narrows his eyes. He steps back, looking down at his watch before tilting his head back and forth, contemplating. He shuffles further away, smirking at me as I balk.

"That's too bad," he *tsks*, crossing his arms over his chest. His pecs push out, the muscles in his biceps bulge. This man is easy on the eyes, and he's all mine. Twisting on his heel, he starts heading toward the exit. Before I can even think it through, I run and jump. I should have known that he would expect it since he twists around just as I make contact. Instead of getting on his back like I planned, he hauls me over his shoulder and smacks my ass harshly.

"Hey!" I shout, swatting him as he walks. "That's not fair." Propping my head on my hand, I pout as he spins around and takes up toward the voyeur rooms. He laughs loudly, the pressure of his shoulders shaking dig into my stomach. His large palm starts massaging my soft bottom through my jeans before he swats it.

"Life isn't fair, suck it up." He sends another few swats to my ass before we finally reach our destination. I expect him to put me down, but he opens the door and swiftly drops me on the bed. I shout in surprise, watching his tight ass walk away to shut and lock the door. He checks the panels to make sure they're not see-through and shuts the curtains.

"Nomad," I breathe, unable to formulate any coherent words.

"You have thirty seconds to get completely naked and present to me." He reaches down and the *beep* sounds.

The timer started.

My clothes come flying off of me, and I pile them on the chair next to the bed. He's extremely particular about having clothes just lying around.

I sink onto my knees and place my hands on my thighs just as the beeper sounds.

"Just in time," he purrs, the sounds of his shoes tapping toward me. His hand lands on my head, petting my hair while my eyes remain on the ground. The knowing clink of his belt rattles in the room before his jeans sag down to his knees.

Reaching to the nape of my neck, he grips tightly at my hair and tips me backward. My mouth hangs open on instinct. His tattooed hand fists his cock, tugging on it tightly as he works himself to my presentation.

"Such a good boy," he coos, dragging the tip over my lips. I stick my tongue out, and he taps himself on it. Closing my mouth around the head, he hisses and steps backward. My jaw opens again, tongue hanging out and waiting for my next move.

He steps back up, dragging it across my face as I take it.

"You look so good with my cock," he groans, dragging the tip back over my tongue. "You'll do good to suck it like your life depends on it but don't make me cum. Understood?"

"Yes sir," I hum, sticking my tongue further out. He slides himself into my mouth with a groan.

"That's a good fucking boy," he grunts, pulling away and snapping his hips forward. The head of his cock hits the back of my throat. I do my best not to gag, letting my stomach clench as he fucks my mouth. Hollowing my cheeks and moving my tongue around, I work him over without moving my body. My hands grip my thighs tightly to avoid grabbing my own dick. He knows how much I love to suck him off and rub one out of myself. That's just the turn on for me.

Opening my eyes, I peer up at him from under my lashes. He's already staring at me with a wicked grin.

"What did I do to deserve you?" I can't help the whimper that slides from me at his sweet words. Usually he's degrading me, which I love to hear, but when he says nice shit? I could cum without even touching myself. Pulling back, I let the saliva drip between us and pre-cum dribbles from the head of his cock.

"I love you," I hum, slurping the spit away. He shakes his head and goes back to using me for his own pleasure. Just how I like it.

"You want me to tie you up? Spank you? Fuck you?" I nod as he makes dirty suggestions. "The bite of handcuffs would be perfect for you." He steps away completely, letting our mixed juices tumble from my mouth and onto my chest. Bending down, he meets me with a dirty kiss. He takes what he wants from me, not even slowing as he yanks me to my feet.

"How would you like me, sir?" I ask, blinking at him innocently. I know he's got a bit of an innocent kink which was just another thing that attracted him to me.

"I can't decide between ass up or cock up," he comments, raking his eyes over my form. Standing a bit taller, I roll my shoulders back and flex my abs. My dick salutes him already, but it jumps at the mention of itself. "I was going to worship your body, make you come a few times. Then you went and decided you wanted to be a brat. Now, do I edge you or do I give you so many orgasms you pass out?"

The saliva that was pooling in my mouth suddenly dries up. Opening and closing my mouth, I probably resemble a fish out of water. I mean, I may as well be at this point. He'll fuck me seven ways to Sunday whether it's by denial or not.

"I even debated on letting you have my ass for the first time," he lilts with false sadness, bringing his hand to my shoulder and dragging it down. It takes everything inside of me to not move, to stay silent.

I'd been begging him for years to let me have his ass, but he always tells me that he is more of a giver than a receiver. There's no denying that he waits for my pleasure, always lets me cum before he lets himself go. I've had good pussy before, but I've not had any ass besides eating it out. I'm missing out, I know.

Goosebumps prickle across my skin as he skims around my cock, not touching it, yet drifting his rough fingers around it. If I wasn't already in trouble, I'd have demanded him grab it and jerk it. He and I both know that I love to be submissive, yet I'm still bratty. I like to say that it keeps him on his toes. He likes to say that it's because I don't listen.

Win, win.

"I've decided," he professes, skating his hand over my stomach and latching onto my throat. "You're going to wish you didn't talk back."

Fuck.

"Wait-"

"On the bed, cock up." He steps back, his arms crossing over his chest in their natural position. While I'm naked, he's still fully dressed. Minus his cock, but just as I go to move, he tucks that back in too.

"Safe word?" He calls as he makes his way over to the toy wall. He begins collecting whips, cuffs, and a spreader bar before he stops. Looking over his shoulder, his brow raises tentatively, hands stopped mid-reach.

"Red," I huff, working my way onto the bed. He hums in acknowledgement, continuing his quest to find shit. Plopping down, I take in the soft material on my heated skin. This shit should be sin, it's so damn good.

"What's your caution word?" His back is to me as I grab my cock, pumping slightly. The muscles ripple in his back while he moves. Drool seeps from my lips before I can stop myself.

"Yellow," I sigh, sliding my hand up my shaft to collect the small bead of pre-cum. He still doesn't turn.

"Your go word?"

"Green." I bite back a moan, which is when he finally seizes up. I can't stop myself as I rub quickly.

"If I turn around and your hand is on your cock, I'm going to deny you so many times you'll pass out before you get permission." I release myself, attempting to dry off the wetness before it's too late.

He glances over his shoulder, disapproval evident. My heart sinks in my chest even though I did it on purpose. I'm the brat, it's my job, yet I hate seeing *that* look on his face. It makes me want to plead for forgiveness.

"Were you touching yourself?" He grunts, stalking over with several items in his arms. Gulping, I debate on whether I want to try and lie my way out of this. If I know anything about my husband, it definitely wouldn't work. Instead, I go the honest route.

"Yes, sir," I hum, leaning up on my elbows. "I couldn't resist looking at you and not taking advantage of watching your body at work. You're too good looking." *Too honest?*

He laughs boisterously, his eyes alight with heat, lust, and humor. There's a small table next to the bed where he places all of his accumulated items. A piece of black silky material shines as he fists it tightly, walking over to me slowly.

"Since you can't help yourself, I should definitely get that under control." Slipping the material over my eyes, he ties it behind my head without catching any of my hair. A pro, he is.

"Please forgive me, master," I coo, knowing he loves it a little too much when I call him that. From the sound, I'm pretty sure he purred.

"I think you're too much of a trouble maker to have that mouth unfilled." Opening my mouth to dispute, he shoves a hollow ball gag between my lips. I protest, but he doesn't listen. Instead, he uses my head being lifted as an opportunity to secure it. My hands instantly move to reach behind my head, but again, he stops me.

"Goodness, baby. You're just in a mood to be completely restricted, aren't you?" I do my best to respond, however, it's all just mumbles and saliva that comes out. Using one hand to contain my two, he slaps metal cuffs over my wrists and binds them to something else. I can't tell what it is, but I don't think I want to know. That's the fun of it.

Grunting, I fight the restraints and twist.

"In the mood to fight?" He growls. A *swoosh* meets my ears right as the leather meets my inner thigh. I must jump a mile off the bed as another hit slaps prematurely on my other leg. Muffled shouts pour through the gag as he continues his myriad.

My cock leaks heavily as my balls draw tight. I'm about to fucking cum just as he stops, stepping back.

"You're liking that a little too much, aren't you?" He snaps, shuffling around. I wiggle on the bed in an attempt to get this damn blind fold off. Sensory deprivation isn't a fan favorite, but I'm never against it. "New plan." A pop of a lid cap then his calloused hand grasps my cock, jerking roughly.

"Mmm," I groan, letting him play with me however he feels. It's far too rough for me to cum, which he knows. He fucking knows that.

Just as I'm about to lose my shit and shout for more, he stops. Again, he fucking backs away from my body.

Soft material cases my ankles, his fingers dancing over my skin as he straps them on each one. After a moment of sitting with my legs propped, he takes the bar and clicks it open several sections. My legs suspend in the air, his hand coming down on my ass a few times before he stops. More clattering then there's a sound of metal on metal. He practically bends me in half as he jerks the bar further up. The warmth of his body is completely gone, so I know he's no longer touching me. Which means that he's tied my legs up to something.

Fucking hell.

"Look at that sweet ass," he exhales, popping the cap on the lube bottle again. "I should take it just like it is. Who needs to be worked up when you're as loose as a whore?" Motorcycles drive in my stomach at his words, my dick jerks at the thought of being taken how he wants me.

"Use me," I beg, wiggling around to get more comfortable.

"Oh baby," he groans, his hands skating over my ass. "You asked for it."

Chapter Fifteen

NOMAD

I watch his gorgeous cock jump at my erotic words. This man is my husband, and I couldn't be more fucking blessed.

Rubbing the lube with my fingers, I don't give him the chance to prepare. I shove into him knuckle deep, listening to the scream he releases around the hollow gag. It's a pleasurable sound with a twinge of pain. A sound I'm familiar with due to all these years of being intimate. Saliva flings out with each shout, my finger slamming into him over and over again. He's still fucking tight after years of brutal fucking.

"You like when I take what I want?" I spit, adding another finger without warning. He nods frantically, his hands balled so tightly they're paper white. A scream rips through him as I work him over, watching carefully at his body language.

"Yes or no?" I mumble, doing a check in. Another frantic nod confirms that we're all good. Pumping my fingers roughly, I lean forward and suck his heavy balls into my mouth. He tries to close his legs, but the bar has him spread so widely they don't even get near each other. Popping off his sac, I lick a line from his asshole to the tip of his cock.

"You're being such a good boy, it's almost enough for me to forget how naughty you were." I coo, planting a kiss to the weeping head. It's an angry red color, damn near purple from the failed releases. His legs start shaking as I twist my fingers and rub a certain soft spot. Back bowing, his moans get higher and higher...

My fingers fall away from his tight hole just before he busts. The frustration is already seeping from his body as he thrashes.

"Were you close? I had no idea," I croon mockingly. A slight sob pushes past his gag, tears soak the material of the blindfold. Another check in, he's good.

Taking my sweet time, I lick from base to tip. He tries to grind upward, forcing his cock into my mouth. I almost let him but decide it'll defeat the purpose and pull back. Another frustrated grunt from him, and we repeat the process.

Over and over again I use his body how I see fit. Alternating between fucking him with my fingers and sucking him off, I take him to the edge before backing off.

At one point, I take his blindfold off and get a death glare from him. It's well worth it, because he remains bound and gagged, enjoying the ride.

After bringing him to the edge more times than I can count, I decide I've had enough playing.

Sitting on my heels, I reach back and pull my shirt over my head. Pax hums his appreciation for my body as he ogles it. He makes it very well known that he admires what he sees. It'll give a man an ego boost, that's for sure.

My belt was undone from before, so all I have to do is pop the button and push them down. Pax sits there with his eyes glued onto my cock, watching as I stroke myself and the trails of the beads of pre-cum that drips from my tip.

"You want that off?" I ask, letting myself go and sauntering over to the bound man. He nods quickly, his eyes pleading with me. "I don't know, you've not been a very good boy today."

Muffled words pour out from behind the gag. I'll put him out of his misery. This time. Reaching behind him, I unclasp the material but hold it in place.

"If you talk back, I'll take my pleasure and forbid you from taking yours until another session. Understood?"

With another quick nod, I remove the slimy silicone. More trails of saliva hang onto the gag as I drag it down his body purposefully. I let the wetness drip down his cock, soaking it for me.

"Please, I need your cock so bad. I want you to fill me up and cum so hard you'll see stars," he starts, spewing different pleas for me.

After a few minutes of toying with him, I again decide it's time for him to get his reward. Even naughty boys get rewards for listening. I pour a generous amount of lube onto myself, rubbing it in and lining myself up. Sinking into him, we both groan our appreciation.

"You're so fucking tight," I grunt, rearing back and snapping my hips forward. Without the muffle, Pax's moans are louder than ever.

Thrust after thrust, I pound this man into the next week. He takes it and pushes back, thrashing his head back and forth as he chants.

"Yes, yes," he repeats, eyes slamming shut.

"Open your fucking eyes," I growl, bending down and biting on neck. They snap open as his mouth drops. "Cum." The single demand is all he needs.

With a piercing scream, thick ropes of cum spurt out of his hard cock. I wrap my hand around him and pump him harshly. It doesn't stop as I bring myself to the edge. He continues to cum as his ass flutters and chokes me.

"Shit," I grunt, my hips stuttering as my movements get sloppy. Finally, my balls draw up, and I detonate. His name explodes from my mouth as I cum harder than I have in a while.

Leaning my head down, we both breathe erratically and try to catch it. Leaning forward, I kiss him softly. Not quite claiming, more of a reassurance.

"That was so fucking good," he sighs, letting his body mold into the mattress. Chuckling, I reach up and undo the bar and his cuffs. I help bring his arms back down before forcing his hips back into proper position. Some people can get kind of locked up. It's not happened to him before, but I don't want to force it and hurt him.

"I love you," I hum, leaning over again for a quick kiss. He smiles into it, wrapping his arms around my neck.

"I love you too." Pulling back, he pecks my nose before shoving me off of him. "Now, time for the aftercare!"

Rolling around bed, I open my eyes and stretch. We both must have fallen asleep, because I can hear the club thumping at full blast. People talk loudly outside of the room. Reaching over, I tap the screen and realize it's been several hours since we came down here. It's also been a while since either of us heard from Aspen. I've not heard from Doc, but that's pretty usual. She's a pretty busy woman, so I wouldn't be surprised. Pax snores softly next to me, the silky smooth sheets encompassing us from our personal scene.

I nudge him gently, and he blinks up, obviously tired. Leaning down, I take his lips with mine in a sweet kiss, one that's not about power or dominance, but about love and courage.

"What time is it?" He mumbles, rubbing the sleep from his eyes.

"Just after five." His eyes pop open, body sitting up quickly.

"We've been busy *that* long?" He asks in shock. I turn my phone and show him the time. "Shit, nothing from Doc?"

"No, I'm sure they're doing whatever it is that helps her recover." I push out of the bed with reluctance, stretching my sore limbs and standing. He whistles lowly, making kissy noises. Rolling my eyes, I resist the urge to turn around and put the brat in his place. It'll have to wait. I want to check up on Aspen before we go out on our newest mission.

Getting dressed is damn near a task. I want nothing more than to jump back in the soft bed and continue my husband's wonderful aftercare. That or eat his ass and fuck him ten ways to Sunday. While I'm absolutely an advocate of aftercare, I have no problems tanning his hide to the point of needing pain relieving creams. Thankfully, he enjoys it too.

"I hope she's okay," he sighs, throwing his clothes on like the room's on fire.

"I'm sure she's fine, Pax." Grabbing the spray, we both work on sanitizing everything. There's a whole crew that will come in, but I prefer doing a cleaning prior to them showing up. Messes happen, and it's just an unnecessary evil I want to avoid hearing about later on.

Chapter Sixteen

NOMAD

By the time we're done, it's pushing six in the evening. Neither Techy or I have eaten lunch, so when we emerge from the BDSM club, we're both starving. The bar area of the MC is hopping with people from all places. There's jacket pickers and regular civilians who just hang out with us to feel cool. Maybe they feel better about themselves if they can get into bed with the big boys.

Widower is sitting with her kids and Hudson at one of the tables further back, just enjoying themselves. I smile when Ophelia spots us, shrieking for Uncle Tee-Tee. We both laugh and make our way over to the table, sliding in with them. She plops herself in Techy's lap, grabbing her cup and hunkering down. He was always the better one with kids.

We order food and watch Widower feed baby Sebastian. Hudson continues talking about some plan he's got for working with the weapons shipments and pushing them across the border. Half-ass listening on my part, I simply play with the back of Techy's hair while he coos at the little girl in his lap. He would absolutely make an amazing dad one day, but biology doesn't work unless we adopt or surrogate.

Yes, I've thought about it. Seeing him hold the club kids really just makes my heart feel full.

"So, how'd your plan go? I've not seen you for a while, so I assumed it went well," Widower says, looking around with a furrowed brow. "Where's Aspen? I thought she was here."

"It actually wasn't too great," I sigh, diving into what exactly happened. Widower hums while we keep the details Rated E, enough for them to get the jist without compromising little ears.

Looking over at Hudson, she gives him a silent squint. The children around us are none the wiser.

"Come to think of it, I've not heard from Doc either." She pulls out her phone with a frown. "I haven't gotten the daily report from her yet. Let me call." Pushing herself out of the booth, she steps away with the phone to her ear. Hudson and Techy work to keep the kids distracted while we all watch with bated breath. Her head shakes as she pulls it away from her, obviously redialing and putting it back to her head. Again, nothing. She strides back, motioning for me to follow.

"We'll be right back," she calls over her shoulder as we both start to walk. Techy and Hudson both shout their 'later's', the kids obviously taking up a lot of their mental capacities. "When was the last time you heard from her?"

"Let me check." Opening the dial outs on my phone, I tap Doc's contact. "It was just after noon when I called Doc, so probably twelve-thirty or so." She nods, tapping away on her own phone.

"Have Techy reach out to some prospects to check cameras," she mumbles, her heeled boots clicking along as we speed walk around. Doing as she asked, Techy quickly reports that the recent patch-in will be doing the checks, some guy named Ravi.

"He's on it," I reply, calling Crusher as we go.

"Boss," he answers, cutting right to the chase. "We're getting ready to put rubber down."

"Understood. How many people are in the detail?"

"Uhm," he pauses, mumbling numbers under his breath. "It looks like there's about twenty men, we have a few front runners. Pretty big gun bust." Cursing, I have him hang on.

"They've got the bust going soon," I say to Widower, knowing she damn well forgot also. In similar fashion, she curses.

"Can he spare anyone?"

"No, they're all vital." She doesn't say anything else, still speed walking down to the clinic. "They're green. We can find others."

"Nevermind, orders are good," I state, hanging up.

"We've got three details out tonight," she sighs, pushing open the clinic doors.

Stepping inside, there's no one around. Heallie is usually hanging around or writing reports for Doc, but she's not sitting at the desk. Widower and I glance at each other, silently agreeing that something's off. Cautiously, we move forward, the only sounds around us are her boots hitting the tile. Other than that, it's a cold silence.

One that doesn't put us at ease.

"Let's stick together," she mutters, pulling her gun from the waist of her jeans. I release my own pistol with a harsh *click* from the holster, keeping my finger off the trigger. For now. Our feet are light on the floor as we keep noises to a minimum, yet we move quickly to start clearing rooms.

One after the other we check rooms, closets, offices, and duty stations to ensure there's no one else here. Just as we're about to turn around, a loud *bang* echoes down the corridor. We don't even think before taking off in that direction, pushing through the room and stopping to see Heallie and Doc gagged and tied up. Heallie's eyes are closed, and I can't quite tell if she's breathing from here. Doc is wide awake, her eyes wide while she shakes her head aggressively. Looking behind us, I ensure that it's just us in the room. Checking everything, we're clear.

Ripping the bandage off, she immediately starts going off.

"It's Ravi, he had some guy with him. They broke into the hospital room and nabbed her. She didn't want to go with them-"

"Woah," I call, holding my hands up. "Let's get you out of the bindings first and see if Heallie is okay." She quickly agrees as we remove the bindings and focus on the unconscious girl. Thankfully, I can see her chest moving and feel air coming from under her nose. Breathing a quick sigh of relief, Doc kicks into action with rolling Heallie into a recovery position, checking on the nasty wound that's leaking blood into her hair.

"This is going to need scans, there may be internal bleeding." Doc stands, turning to walk away. "I'll get the machine running. We can talk once she's in." Turning on her heel, she quickly runs to the other side where there's the big ass machines we may or may not have gotten from cartel jump. Either way, it works.

"What the actual fuck," Widower huffs, grabbing under Heallie's arm and pulling her upward.

"Probably should wait until we have a gurney or something," I suggest. She whips back to look at me with a glare. "Or not, nothing crazy." With another huff, she just about drops Heallie and grabs the life board thing off the wall.

"Better, your highness?" She quips, rolling the unconscious nurse onto the body board. My eyes avert to the ceiling.

"Just get moving." Hauling her up, we take her and help Doc situate her onto the table. Shooing us away, we step out and wait in the viewing room.

"Did she say Ravi?" Widower asks, pulling her phone out. "Because I'm pretty sure we have a Ravi on the tech team..."

"Shit!" I bellow. I whip my own device from its confines and dial Techy. My leg bounces as I wait for him to pick up, only for it to go to voicemail. Redialing, I wait. Again, voice mail. "Techy isn't answering."

"Go check on him. I'll wait here." I take off before she even finishes her sentence.

Chapter Seventeen

TECHY

H udson and I trudge the kids up to their suite since it's close to bedtime. Ophelia ate most of my food, but I'm not one to complain. If their party-pooper of a dad wasn't there, they'd have been loaded with sugar. Minus the infant, he would've just been wound up with a loud toy or something.

"Alright kids. Axel and 'Phelia, teeth," Hudson orders, pointing them in the direction of their bathroom. Neither one of them talk back. They simply do what is asked of them. She wiggles from my arms, dropping a kiss on my cheek before taking off.

"Seb needs a bath tonight," he laughs, looking at the formula-spit up covered infant. A pungent scent wafts off him, and I have to force down the gag. He's definitely stinky.

"Have you heard from Widower?" Trailing behind them, I've decided that I'm going to help. It's not too often that I get to wind them up after Hudson tells them to calm down.

"No, but that's not unusual. She's a late owl and likes to spend time with the guys every few nights." He shrugs, collecting a towel and the small caddy for Sebastian's bath.

"I thought she did that last night?" Again, he shrugs.

"She's a big girl. I don't care if she's out late as long as she's back to give the kids hugs and kisses before bed."

"You're too good of a dad," I laugh, shaking my head. I know I'd have popped a socket ages ago. He chuckles with me as he works to get the bath going for the infant.

We chat while he gives the bath, letting the two older kids come and sit with us. Axel talks about his day at school and how he's going to learn more than his mom. He's vowed to be the MC's best president. We all salute him because the job sucks ass.

When Widower was out after having the babies, Crusher, Nomad and I all decided to split up duties. It was a fucking fiasco. She usually only gets help from Hudson, so kudos to her. I don't want her damn job.

Ophelia talks about how she's got a bit of a crush on one of the boys in her class. Hudson was not particularly pleased, that's for sure. Sebastian simply babbled away, cooing with everyone as they went.

After the water starts getting cold, Hudson gets everyone shooed out of the bathroom.

"Where's mom?" Axel asks with a big yawn. Furrowing my brows, I realize I've been here for over two hours already. I should have heard from Nomad or Widower by now.

"Not sure, kid. Do you mind calling while we get situated?" He wraps the baby in a fluffy towel, kissing and blowing raspberries into his cheek.

"Sure." Stepping out, I dial her number only for it to go straight to voicemail. Checking the signal, it doesn't appear to be jammed. Trying again, it's just static before it goes to the recording. Huffing, I try calling Nomad and Ravi, neither of them answer.

Scrolling through my contacts, I call Crusher.

"Yeah?" He grunts, his voice low.

"Have you heard from Widower or Nomad?"

"It was a few hours ago. They didn't say what it was, just asked if there was manpower. There's about three groups running tonight."

"Shit, if they kept me in the loop, I'd know that," I sass, running a hand through my hair. "Do you think they went on one of the missions with another group?"

"No, it seemed like it was for something else," he pauses, then shots ring out before his line goes dead.

"No luck?" Hudson calls from the bedroom.

"Nah, I'm going to go check on them. Lock the door behind me," I call, slipping back into my shoes.

"You'd never know that I once ran a club," he harrumphs, walking toward me.

"Yeah, ran it into the ground." His fists clench while I laugh, dancing out the door quickly.

"Be safe, yeah?" He calls, watching as I stride toward the main room. Throwing the bird over my shoulder, he laughs. I hear the lock click into place, solidifying that I'm not truly alone.

Am I scared? A little. It's eerily quiet for a club that tends to be jam packed. No noise reverberates up the stairs, no laughing or sounds of fucking. Just...air.

Checking my phone again, there doesn't seem to be a jammed line, and it didn't sound like a com failure when I tried calling earlier. Lines that get fluxed out by signal blockers tend to sound like white noise static.

Another shitty scenario adds to the mix of my fears because I've called three different people, none answering my damn call. Then I reach out to one of the guys who aren't even in the club right now and they answer. Which means, there's one of two instances happening right now.

One, they're fine and just ignoring our calls because they're busy. This one is not as often as people believe. It's truly important for us to ensure we're all safe. So, this one is concerning none-the-less.

Two, they're not fine and they're dead somewhere in a ditch.

For my brain capacity, there's no in between.

Slipping into the club area, it's pretty deserted. There's only a few guys milling around who weren't chosen to go out on runs. Run days tend to be the slowest, but not always. This mission? Payday. No one is at the bar, only two guys playing pool and one guy making out with his ole' lady in the corner. Other than that, there's no one.

Walking to the bar, I wave to the tender who smiles lightly. She's new, not someone I remember seeing before, but an unfamiliar face none-the-less.

"What can I get started for you?" She asks, throwing the rag over her shoulder and propping her palms on the bartop. I take in her features, analyzing her from the employee profiles. Maybe one of the prospects did her paperwork, and I just signed the dotted line. Sitting down, I level her with a stare.

"Vodka soda." She nods with that small smile, turning around and making the drink. I debate on getting straight to the point or not. She seems like the type that could appreciate it.

Fuck it.

"Anything else I can get for you?" She questions, plopping the thick glass on the counter. Smirking, I bring the glass to my lips.

"Information," I state, taking another swig. "Have you seen Widower or Nomad around lately?" Her eye twitches, but she keeps her strong smile placed on her face.

"I think I saw them a few minutes ago. Nomad came steam rolling through here." She points to the stairs then drags her finger toward the main door.

Humming, I take another slow swig. The liquid sloshes around as I tip it around. She watches me closely, brows furrowed like she's in confusion.

"Was he still wearing his bomber jacket? He probably forgot to take it off before he went and tortured someone," I laugh, lying right through my teeth. Nomad doesn't have a bomber jacket. They're too...preppy.

"I think he was wearing it," she giggles, rolling her hair between her two fingers. "It had red marks on it, so he may have forgotten. These men tend to be so ditzy." Furrowing my brow, I try to make sense of her words. Ditzy? That's more how she's acting right now.

Fuck all, I'm not a fucking executioner. Gathering information is a lot harder than it sounds.

Sighing heavily, I drop my line of sight to the counter top, swirling the liquid around in the tumbler. I catch sight of something sitting at the bottom. Digging my finger into the glass, I bring out a mostly-fizzled-out pill.

She's drugging me.

Jaw dropping, I glance up at her only to see the barrel of the gun glaring back at me.

One barrel or two? I can't tell. They're getting pretty blurry, maybe there are three of them. No, that can't be. I know there's only one of her, which would make one gun. Which one is her though? Who is she? Opening my mouth to protest my sudden quadruple vision, I can't seem to get the words out into the open.

My eyes fall shut, and I work to keep them open, only to realize that they won't move.

They're stuck shut.

I can't scream, I can't call for help.

Nothing.

I'm nothing.

"Nighty night," she mutters with a wink. Before I can even muster a question or retort, my limbs grow heavy and my body slumps. Slamming onto the floor, I know I should feel it. My body should at least be groaning in pain, but I don't feel anything. It's numb.

I'm numb.

Chapter Eighteen

Aspen

"Y**ou'd** go for a lot of money," he tsks, dragging the knife through my tangled hair. When it catches on a knot, he eases the metal out of it without yanking it out.

"She would," Stephan agrees, sitting back on his seat. He swirls the liquor in this goblet before taking a hefty gulp. What the fuck is this? The 19th century?

"But, she feels too good for us to ship her off again." Ravi stands, walking over to where Stephan is sitting. His large hand rests on Stephan's shoulder. Leaning down, he whispers something into his friend's ear before taking a step back.

"What do you think, Charlie? Care to take the whore for a spin?" Stephan asks, setting the giant cup on the table and lifting himself up. They all stalk toward me, their eyes filled with nothing but hatred and lust. It's not hard to see what they're thinking.

Yanking on the chains that hold me bound, I wrestle to free myself. Metal bites into my skin where my flesh is thin from malnourishment.

"They're not going to save you, little one," Charles smiles, his perfectly straight teeth slowly getting that ugly yellow hue.

"One day I'll be gone, and you'll fucking regret everything!" I scream, thrashing against my restraints. In perfect time, they laugh at me and my continued failures to escape.

I don't even know how long it's been. I hardly sleep, so tracking through rest is near impossible.

"You're waiting for the impossible to happen. Don't worry, we'll keep you right where you belong. Under us." All three of them pounce, my head slamming into the table harshly and knocking me unconscious.

Why the fuck do I always dream about the craziest shit? Then, add the worst headache to follow. Is it weird that I swear I can feel the hollow of my eye pulsating?

Groaning, I try to rub my temples, bringing my hands up to my head. Other than...they don't move. Another attempt to pull my arms up, but they're stuck.

Okay, maybe it's just sleep paralysis. The demons can't get to me if I can't see them...shit, yes they can. Taking a few deep breaths, I strain my muscles to get my arms up. Rattling echoes through my brain, almost like chains on concrete.

Flinging my eyes open, I go to sit up, only to realize I can't fucking move. My head doesn't even rotate. When I try to drop my jaw, it doesn't drop. Using the zero mobility I have, I flicker my eyes around the bare room. There's not a lot that I can see. Between the darkness and the concrete ceiling, I'm not missing much.

"Ah, look who decided to join us." The warm blood in my veins seems to freeze over with his words. Footfalls slap against wetness, the *splash* from each step. Now that I focus a bit, I can hear the slight trickling of liquid. A dripping noise.

It's peaceful. Something I can focus on when I endure more life-changing pain.

"Deciding to be silent now?" Ravi spits, the splash of his saliva hitting my cheek. Instinctually, I go to wipe it away, but the chains on my arms keep them exactly where they are.

"You'd never know she was the same bitch who tried to run," Charles cackles, rounding next to Ravi. From what I can tell and feel, I'm splayed in a star shape on a metal table. Some kind of contraption keeps my head still while chains hold my limbs.

"I can tell she's in there somewhere," Stephan coos, running something dull over my cheek. Flickering my gaze, I catch the glint of a knife in his hand. Everything in my body is screaming to run and hide, get out of there as quickly as possible.

My survival instincts from before? They're screaming at me not to make a sound and be perfectly docile, just as they liked when I was in captivity last time.

The collection of saliva sticks to the back of my throat, forcing me to swallow heavily. Thinking back to my short couple months with the club, I've come to realize those guys have nothing in comparison to Charles, Stephan, and Ravi.

Nomad would help me with literally anything, Techy too. Crusher taught me how to aim and shoot a guy to the best of his ability since the student—me—was not very good at it to begin with. Maggie showed me the accounting and treasury portion when she saw that I was about ready to spoon my own eye out from boredom. Even Widower, the club president, took me under her wing to help me.

They sought out help for me. Gave me a home and asked nothing in return.

I was a coward to think that they were dangerous now that I'm staring right back at my past.

"We lost her." No sooner than I can bring myself to the present, a white hot burn cascades from my rib cage. These assholes only prey on my sounds, the screams of pure torture and agony. So, I stay mute. When I sat down with Nomad once, he explained why I was being preyed on. Maybe not the official reason, but he gave really good points as to why they may have kept at it so long.

"Being involved with the club can be...complicated," he suggests, avoiding eye contact. Narrowing my eyes, I withhold the urge to swat at him.

"And?" I drag. My elbows drop onto the table with a clatter, startling him.

"And nothing," he mutters as he swings back his beer. "Nothing, I don't know why I said that."

"The fuck you don't," I snap before I can catch myself. Covering my mouth quickly, my eyes get as wide as saucers. "Shit, I didn't-it's not-fuck, I'm not-"

He booms out in laughter, shaking his head. "Cobra, it's fine," he chuckles, resting his hand on mine.

"Cobra?"

"Cobra's are significant to death and rebirth, depending. We've decided that your club name will be Cobra."

"I have a club name?" I wonder as my heart picks up speed. "Wait, you're trying to get me off track!" His hands fly up in surrender while he tries to pass off a look of innocence. The look isn't working.

"No clue what you're talking about."

"Just tell me," I grunt, my nerves starting to grate.

"Well, for one, when you plead for them to stop, most sickos like to hear it when their victims are begging for mercy. Did you do that?"

A shudder racks down my spine as I recall briefly and nod.

"Yeah, that'll do it. Also, they just like to hear when you cry and scream." I open my mouth. "Don't ask questions you don't want the answers to." My mouth rightfully closes.

"So, you're saying that I was in captivity for so long because I begged?" I ask skeptically.

"Not necessarily, but it probably didn't help anything."

"Well," I state, crossing my arms over my chest. "If it ever happens again, knock on wood, I'll be sure to be as silent as humanly possible."

"Fucking whore!" He screams, a blunt force smashing into my stomach. I gasp for air as I'm yanked from my vision. Even struggling to breathe, I refuse to make too much noise. Only as much as I need, nothing more.

"She got some confidence," Charles snarls, his lip twisting animalistically. "We'll have to fuck that right back out of her."

The first thought in my head is to scream and plead with them to stop. For them to just leave me alone, that I'm useless to them. But, as I refer back to the talk I had with Nomad, I decide that they can do whatever they fucking want.

Once I'm free, I'll ensure that they never see the light of day again. Then, I'll make sure Nomad and Techy know exactly how I feel. I can't imagine dying without at least being able to say goodbye.

Chapter Nineteen

NOMAD

Bounding back into the club area, there's no one here. I look around, not seeing any traces of people. Looking down at my watch, it's just after midnight. Have Widower and I been downstairs that long? Not only that, but it's usually pretty busy this time around. There are three teams currently on runs. Either way, it's never *empty*.

I try calling Techy again with no luck. Finally, I call Hudson who answers on the first ring.

"Jesus fucking Christ," he growls, surprising me. "I've been trying to get a hold of you guys for *hours*. What the fuck?" And one of the bosses is not happy. Oops.

"Widower and I got stuck in the clinic. Doc and Heallie were roped up. Heallie might have some other profound injuries, it's unclear right now. I came looking for you guys because the lines weren't working downstairs."

"Techy went looking for you guys a couple hours ago," he states, agitation clear in his voice. "If you both would have looked at your phones, you'd have seen that I sent out an email to the members because I was concerned. He was supposed to call in by now."

"What do you mean, call in?" I ask, running a hand through my hair. Sitting on the barstool, I lean over it with a heavy sigh. Shit just got real.

"I mean exactly what I said. Do I need to spell it out?" He huffs, shuffling around on his end. "Techy went to look for you. You took too long. He was supposed to call me. He didn't. I got worried. I called you. You didn't answer. I called my wife who also didn't answer. I sent an email due to his whereabouts," he states condescending, almost like he's speaking to a fucking child. If it were anyone else, I'd have ripped them a new one. He would understand, but I don't think either of us are in the mood for it right now.

"When did he come looking?" I put him on speaker and get the notes app, I need to start a timeline.

"Around nine."

"From your suite?"

"Yup," he sighs, obviously just as confused. "Then I started getting worried around ten. I'd called you both and didn't hear back. I debated on calling Crusher or one of the other guys, but it wouldn't have helped since they're all out."

"Do you remember Ravi?" I question logging into Techy's software.

"Honestly? No. He doesn't sound familiar, but I don't deal with recruitment. That's the wife." A slight laugh slips out, and I cover it with a cough. "Who did he work under?"

"Techy." Hudson hums in understanding. "Doc said Ravi was the one who tied them up. Aspen got taken and-"

"Woah, you should have started with that!" He exclaims, shock evident in his tone. "What do you mean? This Ravi guy abducted her?"

Smacking a hand to my forehead, I take a deep breath. It's late at night. I probably woke him up. It's fine.

"That's what Doc said." Looking around, the place is cleaned already, as if they had completed closing duties. "Who was on shift tonight at the bar?"

"Uh, let me look." More shuffling and mumbling. "A newer girl named Stanley."

"A girl named Stanley? Doesn't that seem odd?" My gaze catches a gleam a few stools down.

"Nah, it's not uncommon for girls to have boy names. Ophelia was almost Ashton," he retorts.

"Let me know if you're able to get hold of him. Call Crusher and tell him that they're to ride home after the bust if they're able. We need man-power."

"Sure thing." We say our quick goodbyes, and I get to my feet. Stepping closer to the shiny glass on the floor, I realize that it's scattered pretty far. I don't know how I didn't see this earlier.

Bending down, there's small trickles of red stuck in between the wooden floor panels. Normally it wouldn't strike up a weird feeling in my gut. Except, as I stare at the small dots and glass surrounding it, I can't help the sinking feeling that settles in me.

White flakes scatter near the tiny shards, like sweep marks that weren't quite picked up. Rushing to the office, I grab a swab kit and a small cup of water. After a few drops absorb the powder, I twist the swab into the liquid and wait. I'll be honest when I say

I've never had to do a damn drug test for a floor before, so there's no telling whether it'll actually work or not.

"Fuck." Positive for LSD. Standing, I take a quick photo of the test and try to send it to Widower, but it bounces. Right as I go to dial her number, Hudson is ringing in.

"We're fucked," he starts, failing the basic pleasantries.

"Hello to you too," I retort sarcastically with an eyeroll.

"Fuck off," he curses, closing a door. "I logged into the server and it looks like someone tried to loop over some of the records. The dumb ass set it for a thirty-second circuit instead of minutes or hours."

"Jesus. Okay, well I've got weird news. The floor in the club tested positive for LSD."

"What the fuck is happening?" He hisses. I can't help the stupid laugh that bubbles from my throat. This shit is ridiculous, that's for certain. "I can't leave the kids. Take photos, check on my wife, and come to the suite when you're done." He hangs up without another word.

Doing as asked, I take several photos of the area and upload them into the cloud for safe keeping. I'm really curious as to what Hudson found.

I double check the doors are locked and confirm there's a lock-down order that was emailed and issued by Hudson. There's nothing else here that would have even been a sign of struggle. Glass on the ground could be anything, let alone with it mixed with blood and fucking LSD. Those three combined? No good feelings come to the surface while thinking about it.

The clinic is the same as I left it. Widower and Doc are sitting in the viewing room while Heallie is laying flat on the bed.

"She woke up mid-scan. Freaked the fuck out," Widower mutters, patting the seat next to her. "It took forever just to get her calm enough to lay back down."

"I'd react the same way," Doc snorts, looking over at me skeptically. "Fuck. The look on your face doesn't bring good news."

"I've got a bit of good news and a lot of bad news. Which first?" Dropping my head into my hands, I force myself not to think that anything bad happened to my husband. He could simply be sleeping with his phone on 'do not disturb'. That's something he's done before, and I wouldn't put it past him for another time. Unfortunately, this feels too damn real. Too close to home for me.

It was just a few years ago when Crusher was taken from us, thankfully brought back whole. While I want to pretend I'm not projecting my fear, I know for a fact that I'm really only terrified because of the incident with Crusher.

"Techy went back to your suite with Hudson to help with the kids. We weren't responding to their calls, so he went looking. Apparently, Hudson's been reaching out to us because Techy's been missing for a couple hours. He didn't hear back from Techy and called a mandatory lock-down." My eyes burn with tears threatening to reveal themselves. Blinking harshly, I keep them at bay.

Barely.

"Appropriate response," Widower adds just as Doc chimes in. "What else?"

"I found glass shards left over as well as a white powder that popped positive for LSD. It was like someone tried to clean it up but was in a rush." I slide through the photos of the scene. Widower grabs the phone, zooming in on the shards.

"You can see where they took the dustpan and then tried to disperse it."

"If you look closer, you can see blood spots in the panels." I move the photo a bit where there's an undeniable splat of blood.

"Is that..." Widower whispers, eyes snapping to mine. All I can do is shrug.

"I have no fucking clue."

Chapter Twenty

 TECHY

"You think doing the mission solo was right?" I hold down my groan, the fog in my brain slowly clearing.

"The fuck do you mean? We *need* him," a female voice hisses with obvious irritation. She's got an extremely high pitch, one that makes my ears ring due to the surrounding metal.

"You're the dumbest bitch I've ever laid. We needed the girl, not him! He'll lead them right to us," the guy snarls followed by a resounding *smack*. I don't need to be fully conscious to know that he just walloped the shit out of her.

As I become more aware of my body, I realize I'm sitting up with my head tilted oddly. Wiggling my fingers, I'm able to gain feeling back in my arms that I now know are tied behind my back. Without wanting to cause a scene, I test the bindings and the knot. The dumbasses put my hands together. Rule number one: never have the captives hands put together.

Well, I don't know if that's the first rule, but in this case it is.

"Just kill her already."

"No, please don't!" She screams, clattering follows with the struggle. It doesn't sound familiar, but I peek my eyes open just to be sure.

It's the girl from behind the bar.

"We asked you to do one simple task. *One.* Then you bring more trouble to our door," a bearded guy snaps, pulling his pistol from the holster.

"Please," she begs, her voice jerking as another skinnier guy pulls her hair back. "I won't do it again, I promise." She continues chanting how she's going to change.

Unsurprisingly, none of them listen.

"One time is too many. You were shit pussy anyway." With that, he pulls the trigger. Her head snaps backward with the force, body staying upright for a split second, then crumbling to the floor.

"Clean this shit up," beard guy grumbles before stomping out of the room. Two guys trail behind him and slam the door shut. Her head pours red liquid from the wound, brain matter splattered around the wall where she was shot. From how she landed and the angle I'm seated, I can see the exit wound and the giant gaping hole in her skull. I have no doubt that it was done by either a .45 caliber hollow point or a .44 caliber magnum.

Squinting slightly in an effort to see better, I can see skull shards scattered around. Just toward the edge of the wall, there's several blond hairs laying around. Some are attached to pieces of skin, some are stuck to the bone, and others are simply just laying around on the blood getting soaked through.

There's a few minor spasms in her hands, but that's something I've heard about from Nomad before. It's right before livor mortis kicks in. I'm not familiar with anatomy, I just know from what my husband has said.

Now that I think about it, I know more than I probably should. Suddenly, shrieking hinges startle me, forcing me to give up my incognito of unconsciousness.

"Well, well, if it isn't the gay supporter," skinny guy sneers. His small hand grabs my jaw, forcing me to look up at them. There's a familiar metallic taste in my mouth. One that I've not been treated to for years. It damn near brings out the side of me that I've kept hidden away for far too long. The side that only Nomad has seen.

Collecting the blood tinged saliva, I reject it quickly from my mouth, smacking skinny guy and beard guy at the same time.

"Two for one," I cheer quietly, smirking dangerously.

For obvious reasons, they're not a fan of my joke.

Another dude that I hadn't been able to really make out before steps forward, grasping my throat tightly.

"You will do right to remember who the fuck you are," he barks, his face close as possible to mine. From the gay slur, I'm half tempted to lean forward and kiss him. Just to give him a taste of his own medicine. Thankfully, I know the consequences of most of my actions and decide against that plan.

"You'll do right to remember not to fucking project your fantasies on me. Just because I take it up the ass doesn't mean I can't fucking give it." Spoke too soon.

Rearing back, skinny dude slams his fist into my jaw. The bone screams in pain, the overwhelming urge to vomit hits like a train, but I refuse. More blood surfaces, forcing me to either choke it down or spit it out.

I decided on the former.

"I say we do a dump drop," third guy mutters, backing up to stand next to beard. Beard hasn't done much of anything since they came back in. He just stands there with his arms crossed, looking over me as I sit in the chair slumped over.

"I mean, he *is* their head tech guy. Without him, they're fucked," skinny snickers with an odd look in his eye. Going out on a limb, I'd say that he's probably not mentally stable.

They continue talking about options for my doom. Beard doesn't chime in with their negotiations. He just looks at me with his eyes narrowed, as if he's trying to assess and read through something. I do a failed attempt at a smolder, one that doesn't even seem to spark a light of humor in his eyes.

Truly the enemy. Sad.

Finally, after having him analyze me for what felt like hours, he speaks up. "That's enough. Discuss that elsewhere."

Dumb and dumber grumble as they show themselves out. Beard stays. He turns on his heel, grabbing the spare chair and positioning it across from me. Looking at him, he's definitely not small. I'd compare him to Nomad easily, maybe even Crusher who has a few inches on Nomad.

"What do you want?" He asks, crossing one knee over the other and folding his arms across his chest.

I look around, unsure what's happening. "Come again?"

"You have three options. One, how much it would cost to buy your silence and disappear into thin air. Two, put a bullet in your head. You choose."

I'm going to have to scrape my jaw off the floor. "I'm sorry. What?" I ask, squinting at him to try and hear better.

With a dramatic huff and an eye roll, he unfolds himself and places his elbows on his knees, hands clasped together.

"You have a tracker built somewhere in your body, I know that. I'm not stupid," he starts, racking his eyes over my form. An involuntary shiver shoots down my spine, not one of the good kinds either. "I'd rather not waste talent. You work for me, pay money for you to disappear. Or, you die."

"How long do I have to decide?" I ask, swallowing the too-large lump in my throat. He takes a glance down at his watch before smirking.

"Let me bring you a little bit of motivation, hmm?" I open my mouth, but nothing comes out. His shoulders roll back as he stands, making his way toward the door. It slams open, the hinges screaming as he reaches out. A rough looking Aspen stumbles behind him. Her clothes are in tatters, her hair matted on her head and crisp with blood. Her face is red, neck bruised purple.

"Let her go," I growl, tugging at the restraints.

"Finally, a reaction," he smirks. Placing a hand on her back, he shoves her forward roughly. She stumbles as she loses balance, her arms stuck behind her as she falls. The metal contraption on her leg twists painfully. Her chin slams into the dirty concrete floor, and it hits so damn hard I can hear her teeth chomp together.

Wincing, I watch blood pour from her mouth. With watering eyes, she stands slowly. Shoulders rolled back, I witness her gaze turn steely even as thick red liquid gushes from different spots on her face.

Her tongue drags along her bottom lip, scooping some of it back into her mouth before she turns and spits the mix at the beard dude. Surprisingly, he doesn't flinch. Instead he drags his finger through the mixture and brings it to his lips. He doesn't release eye contact as he sucks it down, licking it like it's the best damn honey.

"You're almost as sweet as I remember," he mutters. Stepping closer to her, she locks up tightly and smashes her eyes closed. The middle of his chest meets the top of her head, but he bends down to be level with her. "Our girl here has been naughty, did you know?"

His tongue darts out, swirling on her throat and licking up the bloody mess. My brows furrow, confusion racing in my brain.

Who is he?

"Awe, did my blood bunny not share who she is?" He laughs against her skin, biting down harshly enough for her to jump and scrunch her face in pain.

"Let me go," I growl again, working my fingers on the tie. He laughs again, his beard soaking most of the pouring blood.

My fingers work diligently on the ties, loosening the knot more and more. It's hard not being able to actually see it, but I have to make due.

I can feel the rope give way, and I ball it in my fist. I can't give myself away just yet, so I keep up the illusion that I'm trapped. I need to wait for the right time, a perfect moment for me to pounce. The shittiest part is that I don't know these guys. Being trained versus using that skill in real world situations are very different.

"She's not only a blood whore, but she's a tight fuck," he laughs, smacking her on the rear end. Gritting my teeth, I have to keep calm. I can't blow up. Not fucking yet.

Chapter Twenty-One

Aspen

My heart hammers in my chest, threatening to explode. I honestly wouldn't be surprised if it erupted right where it sits.

Time has passed, that I know of, but I'm not sure how much. It could be days or hours. No windows, watches or clocks give me a set schedule. When my three tormentors come into the room, they're always in different clothing. It's hard to determine if they're in new clothes because of torture sessions or because it's a different day.

While I've had slight down time, I can't help the places that my mind wanders. Nomad and Techy are the two main subjects of my imagination. There are points where I lay here that I debate whether they truly existed, or if it was all a dream. A dream that happened so fast, then I was awakened by my worst nightmare.

It's almost entirely an out-of-body experience at this point. I'm living this torture, yet I'm simply not *here*. When they use me for their own pleasure in whatever way they deem, I'm not thinking about them. My happy place is back at the club.

Satan's Wheels MC quickly became my sanctuary. A place where I knew I could call home. It didn't matter that I didn't have anyone else to call, no one to rescue me. They rescued me from myself a few times. If they wanted to know something, they asked. If I wasn't ready to share, they didn't push me.

Gosh, I'm getting sappy.

Tears burn the back of my eyes as I think back to the wonderful time I had with them. It's hard to believe that those two men quickly became someone I could rely on. Especially since I knew men were the reason for my hurt, my tears, my scars.

Nomad and Techy took on the challenge of my trauma and helped push me past it.

I damn near succeeded too.

All that was left was for me to tell them how I felt about them. How much I really wanted to keep them in my life. They were constantly touching me, checking in on me, making sure I was okay. I know they felt the same, but Widower already said they wanted me to be on my own timeline. Right when I was ready to take that next step, I got struck with a stroke of bad luck.

Unfortunately, that seems to be my entire life story.

Back luck.

Ravi slams into the room with a huge smile. "Get the fuck up." I don't have time to process as he strides over to me and yanks me off the bed by my hair. My entire body screams as he throws me around like a rag doll. Silence is my only key for survival. Or it could be a fast track to my death.

I'm not going to be picky.

Stumbling a few steps, he tugs me through the doorway and down the hall. A door slams open, and voices carry down the hall as we get closer.

Stephan and Ravi shove me through the doorway, and my face meets the floor. Ears ringing and eye sight blurring, I do my best to stay conscious. My teeth slam together, the familiar tinge of iron leaks onto my tongue.

The thick liquid trickles down my chin, trailing onto my chest and into my tattered shirt. In an effort to slow it, I lick my bottom lip and get as much off without moving. *His* presence is heavy behind me as he moves my hair. I can't hear what he's saying over the white noise in my ears.

Techy struggles against the bindings, his face contorted in anger as he yells something. My head gets light as I lose more blood, then Charles darts his tongue over my flooded flesh. I don't think my spine could get any straighter at this point.

"Think she could make the gay guy straight?" Charles mutters, his breath hitting the wetness and shooting a tingle down my rod-hard spine.

"She doesn't have a magic pussy," Ravi snorts, twining his fingers through my hair and yanking my hair backward.

"Then let us go!" Techy snarls. The three men laugh at his failed attempts. Hands grip my shoulders and push, coercing me onto my knees.

Stephan moves swiftly over to Techy, unbuttoning his pants and fighting with him to get them off. With a swift kick, Techy manages to sack Stephan in the nuts.

Even I wince.

"You fucking-" Techy's fists fly from behind his back, swinging on Stephan. A gun cocks from behind me and a hard metal pressed into my tattered hair. I can't help the sob that pushes past my lips. I'm unsure if the tears are from relief or fear.

Probably both.

A wicked grin plasters onto my man's mouth, his bloody teeth revealed.

My man?

"You'd be right to stop, Techy," Charles demands, nudging me with the gun. Losing balance in my kneeled position, I tip forward and face plant into the ground. Again.

"What are you going to do?" Techy taunts, grabbing the third wheel of the trio. Stephan trips over himself as he's now forced to stand. Locking an arm around the man's throat, Techy pins his front to Stephan's back. "Shoot her?"

"Damn right," Ravi snaps. He jumps forward, but Charles holds an arm up to stop him.

"You shoot her, you lose income. Let me go," he snaps. I attempt to look up at Techy, but my neck doesn't tweak that way. Biting my lip, I keep from screaming at them all.

Nomad once told me that they'd do anything for me. Keep me safe, and if anything ever happened, they'd do everything in their power to return me to them.

Sitting here right now, it's hard to believe that anything he said was true.

"How do we know that you're not going to bring back the mob? Get your revenge?" I can't help fissure that tears in my heart. It tightens painfully, and I jolt without warning. A boot lands on my head, keeping me from trying to move again. I grit my teeth, forcing myself to stay silent.

"You think we cared about her?" Techy scoffs. I assume from the sounds of choking that Stephan is still in a head-lock.

I want nothing more than to believe Nomad's words. There's so much more to it than this. His words ring through my head over and over again.

Just more people who made promises they couldn't keep.

"She was just a time sake. Honestly, we lost interest when she wouldn't put out," he laughs, though it's strained. The slight crack gives me just a tinge of hope.

"Oh, we're familiar," the three goons cackle. Wouldn't it be stupid to compare them to that wicked witch? "That's why we force it. She doesn't know what she wants, we just have to give her a little *nudge* in the right direction." The boot lifts as a hand weaves through my tangles. Jerking backward, my neck strains with the effort to stop from snapping in half.

"Unfortunately for her, we can't keep her much longer," Ravi sighs, dragging a blade down my throat. "She's been causing far too much trouble."

"We did the 'get to know her' method. You could've tried that," Techy suggests, meeting my eyes. There's several emotions that cross through them, but I can't read into any of it.

Fog covers my eyes as my brain spins. The loss of blood seems to be catching up. There's suddenly a double in the men in front of me, and the only thing keeping me upright is the hold on my hair.

Blinking gets slower as white dots invalid my vision.

Chapter Twenty-Two

NOMAD

Pacing the floor, we wait for an update on Techy. About an hour ago I got an odd call from an unknown number, one that I was baffled to have gotten. It was elusive and pretty perverse, but I wasn't going to question it. They said they were bringing him back to me. That's all I care about right now.

"Where are they dropping him?" Hudson asks, parking himself in the chair next to mine. The one I occupied for I decided there's too much pent up energy for me to stay put.

"They didn't say," I start, running my hands through my hair.

"I've got a tracker on him," Robo calls, his fingers fly across the keyboard as numbers shoot onto the screen. A little red dot dances around. "The call was long enough for me to get the intel. I'm sending the coordinates to you now, it should allow you to monitor his movement as you go." Phones ding around the room, several members pulling their devices out for the tracking.

"We need to be there when they drop him off," I warn as eyes land on me. "We also can't be seen. If I got the message correct, we're already on thin ice."

It took me about ten minutes to realize that Techy's speech was actually a code. When I saw it was from him, I immediately knew to record the conversation. Widower and I played it over and over again, debating if there was anything to even get from it. Then, Robo and Appa came into the room, heard the ques and started drilling into it.

Don't ask me how they did it because I'm definitely not the smart husband in our marriage. The two nerds worked for only five minutes before deciphering the message.

"Aspen alive, here, underground," they agreed. How'd they celebrate their victory? By tracking Techy's phone to the place where they–hopefully–kept them hostage. By hopefully, I mean that we need to find Aspen.

Fast.

I'm first to volunteer on the rescue mission and a few other executioners join. Crusher volunteers as well, but Widower winks at him and holds him back. Something about coming up with a game plan. At this rate, I honestly don't give a rat's ass.

I just want my husband back.

The dirt lot is practically ice as we pile out of the club, but we were sure to salt the main areas. Thankfully, the road crews are diligent about maintaining roads around here. "You all got it pulled up?" I call out, the roar of machines cutting out my voice. Several thumbs up, and we're ready to ride.

Turning the key over, I flip the switch. My beast vibrates in happiness underneath me, purring as I kick up the stand and take off. A slight fish-tail onto the road, then I open the throttle.

"Com-over," Robo calls over the gearset, startling me slightly. With an over exaggerated eye roll, I respond.

"You don't need to end your sentence with 'over'," I scoff, watching the darkness envelope us. The lights on our bikes cut through it, but the moon doesn't do much to help. Crickets damn near chirp as I wait for a response. After a moment, I realize, "over," I grumble.

"Great! You're coming up on the joint turn. It might be bumpy, so slow down and fall back a few lengths, over." My irritation slowly dwindles as the idiot plays astronaut from afar.

Grabbing the clutch, I kick down a gear and decrease the speed. The quiet surrounding us could easily carry the overwhelming purrs from the bikes, so staying back a bit helps keep them from anticipating us.

The ride is long, nearly an hour as we cruise down backroads and plains. I bet it'd be really pretty when the sun is out. If he's not too haunted by this experience, I might just take him on a ride through here. Hopefully he wouldn't even remember this area since it's pitch black.

"It looks like he's stopped, over," Robo announces, keys on his keyboard clacking annoyingly. Sucking on my teeth, I slow even more until we're at a stand-still.

"How do we know when to go?" I ask, flipping my visor and scanning the surrounding area.

"Techy will start walking. He's under the impression that's what he'll need to do anyway."

"What if they're still with him when he moves?"

"When has that ever stopped you?" Robo snorts.

"Touche," I mutter, putting the kickstand down. Several guys follow suit, shutting off their bikes and walking around. After a few minutes, I see movement in the distance. It puts me on edge as

I turn back to the phone. The red dot moves slowly, but it's on the path toward us.

"I wonder if that's him," one of the guys asks, squinting to get a better look. Flicking on the headlight, I notice the same clothes Techy was wearing when he was abducted. Without thinking, I take off in his direction. The guys shout after me, but I don't care.

It's him. It's fucking him.

His knees buckle as he drops to the ground, a quiet sob reverberating around the otherwise quiet forest. Snow covers the ground thickly, his body shivering from lack of protection. Dropping to the ground with him, I scoop him into my arms and hold him as close as I possibly can.

"I thought I lost you," I whisper, tightening my grip on him. His shoulders shake as he cries harder, arms wrapping around me as he uses my chest as a pillow. Not that I mind.

"We'd better get going," Razor calls, stepping toward us cautiously. "It's great to have you home, but we need to move. We don't want to get caught out here if those guys are lingering."

Techy nods, wiping his nose on my jacket before standing. I lace our fingers together, not even giving him the option to walk without me.

We make it back to the club in one piece, though Techy is shaking like a leaf. I'd given him my jacket before we left, but I think it's all of the adrenaline from the past couple days. Our wonderful club president bounds out of the doors, snatching Techy up and giving him the biggest hug. She's not an overly touchy person, so I know this means quite a lot.

"We have a lot of work to do," Widower states, leading the parade back into the house.

"Can I get an hour or so?" Techy asks quietly. He stops just inside the door, looking around as if he'd never been here before.

"I'm going to take him upstairs," I tell her, not giving him an option. "Leave your phone so the other guys can work on it."

"Oh, it's fine, I can do that-"

"Babe, phone," I demand, my hand outstretched and waiting. I can see the contemplative look in his eyes before he relents. Digging in his pocket, he holds his phone tightly in his fist. I'm honestly surprised they didn't smash it or something. Which, we're going to wipe clean and check for bugs. Even then, it may be too late since none of us thought about it before we left.

Quirking a brow, he finally sighs and slaps it into my hand. A bright smile is one of his rewards, handing it over to Robo as they welcome Techy back.

They surround him tightly, giving him praise and welcoming him back home. The man looks ready to either fritz out or fall asleep. On occasion, his eyes will snap to me for help in which I'll simply hold my hands in surrender. So far, that's earned me two death glares.

Looking at my watch, it's been over thirty minutes. I decide to be a good husband and step in to be his savior.

"Alright, he needs some space," I command, using my size to shield him away from everyone. "Go assist your president with anything she needs. We'll be back later." With that, I lace my husband's fingers through mine and drag him up the stairs.

I can hear a near-silent sigh of relief as I pull him away from everyone. Knowing him, he was absolutely overwhelmed with the amount of people that were there to greet him. He's not one for the fanfare, but it's also good for his self-esteem to see that the club truly does care for him. More than the usual appreciation for keeping their virtual foot-prints clean.

"Do you want to talk about it?" I whisper, throwing my arms around his shoulders and pulling him tightly against me once again. He shakes his head. It's a decision I can respect, so we stand there in silence. The heavy beat of his heart pumps between us, pulsing against me.

"I love you." Pinching his chin gently, I tilt his head back. We stare into each other's eyes for a few moments. He's a true beauty, one that I'm lucky to have come across at such a young age.

He's absolutely my soulmate.

A lone tear trails down his cheek, a smile slightly tugging at his lips. Using my thumb, I drag the wetness away gently.

"I love you," he mutters back. His hands reach around my waist, tugging my shirt out of my pants.

"We shouldn't," I shutter, not meaning a damn word. I need him more than anything, but I don't want to be the reason he has tormented thoughts. I don't even know what they did to him while they had him.

"There's a lot that I need to say, a lot that needs to happen, but I need this. Just a few minutes. You and me." How the fuck can I say no to that? Leaning down, I plant my lips over his, molding gently. He melts against my body as a light hum escapes his chest. It's like a purr, except his hips press harder against mine.

"Shower," I gasp.

Chapter Twenty-Three

 TECHY

His hips crash against mine as we stumble toward the bathroom. Lips smacking, hands roving, neither one of us seem to get enough of each other. If anything, the fact that I was gone for a couple days makes me extremely grateful to have him in my life.

Yes, I know there's looming danger with Aspen, and it's carved into the back of my brain. If I go into that without a clear head, I may as well be useless to the team. My lack of giving up my phone said it all.

"Stay with me," Nomad chides, his large hand landing on my ass and squeezing. Nearly slamming into the door frame, he pins me against the wall and devours me whole. Maneater, my husband is. Not that I'm complaining.

"I'm here." I inhale harshly when his hand goes from kneading my ass to stroking my straining erection through my jeans.

"No, you're not," he growls, leaning down and biting harshly into my neck. "You're still thinking about what happened. The team is working on everything. Take time for yourself." Nodding, I melt into the burly man who is literally my heart and soul. Fingers moving swiftly, and my pants are suddenly around my ankles. My brain doesn't even get a second to catch up before he's on his knees before me, his shirt discarded somewhere else. The muscles on his shoulders ripple as he situates himself in front of me.

"You don't-"

"Shut up already," he growls, latching his mouth around my pulsing length. I swear my thoughts even stutter as he flicks his tongue over the head. His rough, calloused hand wraps around it easily, stroking the length that doesn't fit all the way in. Knuckles white, my fists ball tightly next to my body.

That apparently isn't the right move.

Popping off, he manages to top me from on his knees. "Fuck my mouth, Pax." Without warning, he grabs my tightly wound hands and shoves them onto his head. Like second nature my fingers open and clasp tightly on the soft strands. The only warning I get is the deep groan that echoes off the walls.

Ever-so-cautiously, I hold his hair and pull my hips back. I let myself rock forward carefully so as to not hurt him.

Another wrong move.

Crack. I yelp as his palm lands firmly on my ass. My grip turns brutal as I accidentally force my cock down his throat. He doesn't look at all surprised from under his lidded eyes, almost as if he was anticipating it.

"If you don't let go, I'll make you," he threatens. I know damn sure he's not kidding.

Rearing back, I ram forward. He chokes loudly, back hunching slightly from the force. Eyes as wide as saucers, I attempt, and fail, at getting myself away from him.

"I almost hurt you," I protest, taking a step back. His hand clutches my dick tightly, tugging me toward him with it. It's a brutal squeeze, one that causes me to hiss between my teeth.

"Fuck. My. Mouth." The demand is there, clear as day. He drags a few fingers through the dripping saliva between my cock and his mouth. He circles a finger around my tight hole and pushes inside.

"Fine," I breathe, reclaiming my lost grip and driving into his mouth. Another similar sound is released from him, but he encourages me by pushing further into my ass. His eyes roll back into his head as he seems to savor me. Sucking me like a damn lollipop.

My sac is heavy with the need to release, but I won't. I want him so deep in my ass that I won't know today from tomorrow.

"Please," I whimper. I take in his watering eyes, drool dripping down his bare chest and onto his jeans. Direct eye-contact has always made me squirm, but seeing this Greek God on his knees for me...I may be dead.

Is this my personalized version of Heaven? I don't even know if it exists, but if this is what it's like, count me in.

"What do you want?" Drew growls, the vibrations traveling down my shaft, into my sac, and up my spine. The involuntary shiver racks through me. His slick finger travels slowly out of me before driving back inside. I can't help but clench on him, imagining that his giant cock is shoved so deep inside of me.

"I want you to fuck me," I demand, surprise evident through both of us as I slap my hand over my mouth. Removing his finger, he stands. A slow smirk creeps over his face as he unbuttons his jeans. Kicking them off, he strokes himself. There's no need, he's long, thick and heavy.

Reaching around me, the shower suddenly turns on, startling me slightly. I'd completely forgotten we were in the bathroom.

"Your knees," I gasp. Tile floors aren't the greatest to kneel on, simply ask the bottom.

"Believe me, sucking you distracted me plenty," he mumbles. Kneading the soft flesh of my ass, he groans deeply. We brush together, another shudder flowing through both of us. Undulating gently, our sensitive shafts jump against one another.

Fingers catching in the ends of my hair, my head is tugged backward. His lips land on mine heavily, our mouths weave and dance. Tongues flicking against each other, he captivates me and kisses me until I can't breathe. Even then, he doesn't let up. Coasting down my throat, he sucks harshly on several spots. One spot in particular under my ear has my knees buckling. I damn near jump into his arms with how good it felt. If his cock was inside of me, I definitely would have came. *Hard.*

As if reading my fucking mind, his hands coast to my ass then to my thighs. Light pressure pushes on the back of them. Throwing my arms around his neck, I don't even get the chance to jump as he pulls me up. The squeal of surprise slips before I can even catch it. He absolutely takes pride in being able to throw me around like a rag doll.

Stepping into the shower, we're immediately taken over by steam. Hot water meets my back, but it's not too much. It feels just right, exactly how I like it.

"Are you trying to get brownie points, mister?" I tease. He shakes his head with a light laugh.

"Yes, sir," he retorts, bringing my lips back to his.

"Well, you do know that shower sex isn't ideal, then?" I question. It's something that so many people think is a real thing. Water isn't oil, and it just makes you chafe.

Unless you have lube in the shower. Like a smart person.

My husband is said smart person.

With another laugh, he sets my feet on the floor before turning me around. I don't get a warning as I'm forced to put my hands on the slippery wall.

"Oops," he exhales. Cool drops of lube meet my puckered hole contrasting the warm water and steam surrounding us. "Guess we'll just have to make due then." I'm about to make a snippy comment when he nudges the head of his thick cock in my entrance.

Brows pinch, mouth dropping, I'm panting and ready for him to bottom out inside of me. In all honesty, I don't think I'll ever get tired of him using me like his own damn pleasure toy.

"Oh, fuck," he grunts hoarsely, one hand clasped tightly on my hip while the other guides him further into me. Stretching me to the max, I cry as his balls slap against mine.

"You feel so good," I croak, reaching behind me to grab onto him. His fingers lace with mine, twisting slightly and pushing it up my back. Our twisted arms rest on my lower back and he uses it for leverage.

He drives in and out of me without abandon, tweaking his hips slightly until he hits *the spot.*

"Yes!" I cry, knees threatening to buckle. Pushing backward, I use the leverage we have to fuck him frantically. The special spot shoots me higher into the sky of pleasure, sitting right on the edge.

"Cum for me," he grunts, reaching around and stroking my pulsing cock. Sparks start low in my stomach, spinning and twining through my nerves. Finally, I shout as he pushes me over the precipice of pleasure harshly. My body convulses, ass fluttering around his cock as he drives roughly into me. His breath stutters, body shudders as he releases deep inside of. I'm still shooting ropes of cum onto the wall as he wrings me dry. His hand doesn't let up, ensuring I've been completely drained.

Pulling away slowly, I can't help the cold feeling that overtakes my body from the loss of him inside of me. It's an odd feeling, one that doesn't seem to happen often.

"You okay?" He asks, wrapping me tightly in his arms. I nod, curling like a cat in his strong grip. There's this heavy feeling in my chest about everything around me. It's like a crushing weight, but I'm also much lighter than when we came in here.

"Let's wash up." He reaches around me, grabbing the washcloth and lathering it with soap. Taking great care with my body, he gently makes sure that I'm taken care of before he even thinks of himself. Fingers dig deeply into my scalp, and I can guarantee that he's trying to avoid a slight drop in my emotions. Widower used to experience them a lot, they were pretty harsh, so I'm grateful mine haven't been that bad. I just tend to get this heavy feeling, that's all.

"I love you." Standing on my tip-toes, I bring his mouth to mine. This kiss doesn't determine who is in charge. No, this one simply says that we love one another unconditionally. Even if it means bringing a third person into it.

"I love you, Pax," he sighs happily, cupping my jaw and pecking across my face lovingly. I laugh and shove him away lightly.

We both wrap in fluffy towels, drying off and relishing in the time we have alone.

"Are you tired? I can ask Widower to give you the night. They probably won't need you until the morning if they're tracking off your phone."

"I haven't slept in a couple days, but I don't want to keep Aspen in that situation any longer." My mind is split between getting her back and the utter exhaustion that threatens to take over my mind and body.

"Like I said, we can rest and set an alarm. They're going to be digging into the phone. There's not much we can do tonight besides allow you to rest." Nodding, we both slip into a pair of boxers. He shoots a quick text to Widower to let her know, and we slip into bed together. Our hair is still wet, but I don't think that's ever stopped us. Bed head is a new trend. If it's not, then it should be.

"Rest," he commands. He clings to me tightly, my head resting on his chest and listening to the soft pattern of his heart beating.

Chapter Twenty-Four

ONE WEEK LATER

TECHY

"There!" Robo shouts, pointing to the dart on the map. Zooming in, we manage to drag the camera to a better angle point. Two guys walk out of the house, laughing and shoving one another. A third trails after them, large and scruffy.

"That's them," I exhale, my chest deflating from the overwhelming anxiety of trying to find her. "Any sign of her?"

"Not from what we can see," he mutters. Clicking quickly, he manages to pull several different cameras onto the screen, flipping between them.

"I taught you well," I admire, pride evident in my throat.

"Only the best." Standing, I round the table and stand right in front of the screen. The location is oddly familiar, but I can't pin-point it. Markers around the area spark something in my mind, like a switch trying to flip over and failing. Until...

"Holy shit," I mutter, pointing to a square in the upper corner. Appa moves around the room with me, waiting for Robo to open it.

"Isn't that the same place they kept Crusher all those years ago?" Several eyes go wide. It's different seeing it in the broad daylight. Everyone went during the night, drove around.

"No," Crusher states, crossing his arms over his broad chest. "That's not it. The buildings aren't quite the same."

"You remember?" Nomad asks skeptically, coming to stand next to him. Crusher just nods. It's like watching him get transported back to the worst time of his life.

"I've been there yearly," he informs, his head turning over his shoulder. "It's similar, but it's not the same area."

"Zoom out," I call. Robo does as asked, and the camera is pulled away again. Again, the spark clicks without recognition. "I swear I know this place."

"You know what?" Hudson starts, taking a closer look at the image. "That looks like the old clubhouse for Satan's Wheels."

I'd completely forgotten that the club had dissolved and merged with the Sinclair's.

"You're right," Widower agrees, rocking Sebastian on her chest. "Why would they choose that only place? It was falling to the ground last time we were there."

"There are cells underground, that's why," I state, shaking my head. "I should have guessed that, but then again, I couldn't see anything until they dropped me."

"Don't blame yourself," Nomad shushes, wrapping an arm around my shoulder. "There was nothing you could have done."

This is a fight he and I have wasted our time on for the past week. If my senses had been higher, better trained for it, I wouldn't have gotten nabbed. I'd immediately assumed that it was fine, that the random girl in the bar was a member. None of the other guys who were gathered around seemed to be stirred one bit.

Gender didn't matter since it was an unfair fight. She had the advantage of drugs on her side. Sadly, I'm the scrawny dude that fell in love with the big burly man. Most people expect me to be able to fight back. It's nearly laughable, because I try my hardest, but I could easily be overtaken.

That was another argument that involved the whole damn club. No one thought to say something about the random chick they'd never seen before. Instead, they were more worried about getting their dicks sucked and fucked. The three guys who lingered around when I was taken seemed to have gotten the same fate as the blond imposter bartender.

Shot between the eyes.

"Enough," he demands, tilting my chin upward. "You keep talking down about yourself, I'll have no choice but to punish you. We don't have time, so you better keep that in mind. Either reprimand you or find Aspen. You choose." He doesn't let me pull away from him, keeping our eyes level to one another. Jerking my chin out of his grip, I can't help the pout that juts my bottom lip.

"Fuck off," I mutter, shoving away from him. Eyes glance between us, several that are suggestive and others that are confused. "Get back to work." They all immediately look away, smirks pulling at their faces as they all attempt to not laugh. It's a shitty attempt, because seconds later, they're all cackling. Sensing the overall embarrassment, my chest flames up to my ears.

"Who is going to take point?" Hudson asks, grabbing the swaddled infant from Widower. Glancing around, it seems the consensus isn't unanimous.

"Widower?" I ask, unsure.

"I think I should," Nomad says, a bit offended that I volunteered someone else.

"Actually," Appa speaks up, hesitation pinching his features. "I think Crusher should." We all glance around, Crusher even looking unsure.

"Second," Robo pipes in. Several glares are shot in their direction. "It's literally his job," he explains. His shoulders remain straight and determined.

"Fine. Crusher is point. I'll be back," Widower huffs, taking Sebastian out with her. It's an awkward exit and we're all unsure what to do for a moment before a loud *clap* moves us back into motion.

"We all know what to do. We ride in thirty," Crusher commands. "Don't wear anything too heavy but stay warm."

Rounding up my group, we start working on gathering mics and testing them for full functioning. It went from plotting to a mad house in mere seconds.

"Tech van is 'round back," Appa calls, strutting inside. His face is bright red from the wind whipping in his face, and I can only hope the guys all have gators or ski masks to shield themselves from the brutal wind.

The sludge has mainly turned to ice, but that's never deterred the guys. I know I give shit to Nomad all the time for it, but he's smart. If anything, he's not willing to risk his precious bike getting hurt.

"Let's get a head start."

"Everyone in position?" Nomad calls over the radios. There's several static replies as we wait for the final signal. "On my count," he mutters over the speaker, rustling and static echoing down the line.

Myself, Robo and Appa are all stationed outside in the Tech van, waiting for the final call. My adrenaline spikes through my veins as they make calls to one another. The guys and I are keeping track of their body cameras and mics to ensure maximum safety.

Right before they showed up, we flew over an infrared camera to ensure everything was accurate. From Hudson's description of the place, it appeared to be the same. Minus the additional explosives they keep hidden away as fucking boobie-traps, there was the body we were looking for. At least, I hope it is. It wasn't moving, but it was still warm all around, so that's a good sign.

Guys call through the mics that they're in position, and five dots dance on the side of the building to confirm. My stomach is heavy, chest tight. If anything goes wrong...

My brain takes me back to when I had to run the tech van with Widower all those years ago. Getting a member of the team back seems to be turning into a recurring trend. One that we're more than keen on breaking.

"Three." My heart races in my ears with anticipation, legs bouncing harshly under the table of the Tech van. Robo and Appa are stationed around me, hacking into the systems of the three men who decided to uproot my life and take an important piece of it with them.

A shout of victory from Appa who confirms the underground explosives are re-geared to our command panel. Two of the traps are on the outskirts by the trees. From the calculations, they're only grass grabbers, a small tuft of ground will move underneath, and is where the damage is. They're equipped to shake harshly, notifying them that they've got company. Which is the move we're trying to make.

"Two." Glancing behind me, the two guys all jerk their heads in acknowledgement. I wonder if any of the guys on this mission are experiencing flash-backs from when they had to rescue Crusher.

Hopefully Crusher is able to lead this with a clear head.

Maybe it wasn't the best idea to make him point on this. I mean, yeah he has a ton of experience and it's his job as Sergeant at Arms to ensure that all members are safe, up to and including conducting literal extractions like we are today.

Green flashes across the screen as Appa sets one of the bombs off. Grass flies out from its roots, the ground rumbling underneath us.

"One."

Chapter Twenty-Five

Aspen

Water pours over my face as I gasp for air. After a moment, they remove the cloth, cackling to each other. Struggling to breath, it's almost as if they know who Techy was to me. That I thought of him as more than a friend. Then he flipped the script and left me here to die.

Alone.

Not that I'm complaining, but I would rather have a quick death than this waterboarding shit.

Perched on the metal table, they have my arms and legs tied down while my head hangs over the edge. Using gravity to their advantage, they put the burlap cloth back over my mouth and nose, and pour. I take a giant lung full of air right before it hits me. Water leaks into my nose, the burning sensation causing tears to sting in my eyes.

It's like I swallowed chlorine.

"Are you ready to tell us?" Ravi chides as the cloth is ripped off. I sputter and shriek for mercy, but it doesn't last. "You could easily be sitting back in your little prison with food, but instead you're holding their information like they're trade secrets."

"I don't know anything," I lie again, shaking the water out of my hair. The weight on the strands puts more strain on my neck, and it's damn near too heavy to move at this point. Time has lapsed around me, I know that much. What I'm completely unaware of is how much time. Everytime I see my three walking nightmares, they're dressed in different clothing. They never come down in sweatpants or anything resembling pajamas, so I can't tell if it's night or day.

"Bitch!" Stephan shouts, thin wood meeting the soft skin of my throat. "You just want to suffer, don't you?" I try again to disagree. The strain on my airway seems to be catching up to me as dots dance in my vision.

It definitely wouldn't be the first time that I passed out.

"Sit her up," Charles grumbles, yanking Ravi away. A fist tangles in my knotty hair. Blood travels away from my face, the heat slowly vanishing. Keeping my eyes shut, I don't want to face them. They were once a part of my not-so-distant past. They've come back to haunt me.

Metal clanks, my legs loosening from their tight hold. I lost feeling in my toes a while ago, but I know they'd get off on that information.

"Get her out of my site," Charles' deep voice rumbles. Goon one and two grab my arms and practically drag me off the table, relishing in the painful groan that pours from my mouth.

The metal fixator on my leg is dirty and the skin around the wounds are bright red, most likely from infection.

Energy is non-existent in my body. If anything, I know attempting to gather my wits will only make them pull harder.

"Maybe we'll enjoy her before we kill her," Ravi snickers. His hip bumps against mine painfully, the bone bruised from being dragged, beaten, and thrown around. They've left me in my clothes from when they nabbed me, though I'm not entirely sure why. It could be some type of sick fascination with how bloody they've become or they just like to know that I'm obviously below them.

Either way, I'm not going to say anything. Something is better than nothing. Then again, I don't seem to have the best of luck.

"I think you're right," Stephen smirks. His rough hand grabs my butt and yanks on the sensitive flesh roughly. From where he's touching, I wouldn't be surprised if there's a bruise that he's purposely pushing on.

They toss me into the room they've deemed as mine. The ground is wet and there's a pungent moldy smell that's taken over. In the middle is a top sheet, then a bucket off in the corner where I do my business. I'm not afforded any luxuries, but at least I'm not chained to the wall.

Stephan comes into the room with Ravi in tow, shutting the door roughly behind them. "Last chance to be a good blood whore. Maybe we'll even let you enjoy yourself if you tell us what Satan's Wheels MC is planning."

I can't help the hysterical laugh that starts in my throat, bubbling out of me before I can stop it. At this rate, I wouldn't be surprised if I'm wholly delusional.

"You think I know anything?" I laugh. I crawl to the sheet and lay down flat. The ground gives my back and neck a bit of respite from the earlier strain. "You heard him when he left. I'm nobody. Why would they give me information then leave me here?"

"What if they planted you here as a mole, to infiltrate us?" Stephan sneers, kneeling next to me. "Oh, I know. We're going to have to do a cavity search, right?" Keeping my face flat, I do my best to steady my racing heart. They can't win.

"Do whatever you need to," I sigh, lacing my fingers over my stomach and staring at the ceiling. Reverse psychology. Let them think they're one step ahead, but if I don't plead against them, it won't be as fun.

Both men turn to face each other, and I keep focus on the stone ceiling. If I look at them, they'll know I'm bluffing. If I'm caught, I'm fucked.

Literally.

"It's worth it. For all we know, there could be a microphone shoved up your ass." It takes every ounce of power in my body not to scoff and snort. I've never willingly let anyone up there, yet they think I let someone plant something that could get stuck?

Count me out.

"We know you'll enjoy it, babe," Stephan says, lying down next to me. One part of my brain is screaming at me to fight back, kick them in the nuts, anything. Yet, the other more logical side is screaming at me to wait it out. Be patient. Ride the tidal wave.

Don't make a ruckus until you're ready to run. Unfortunately, with the state of my leg, I can't go too far. Trapped once again. Nothing new.

Before I can even blink, my shirt is being torn in-half from one of the holes they'd made previously. My bra manages to hang on by a thread, yet that doesn't seem to stop them.

Staring at the ceiling, I try to dissociate.

Their grimy hands grab and tug while my body naturally fights back. I'm not even sure what's happening, it's almost this out of body experience. Again.

Looking around, I swear I'm seeing this from someone else's view. I can see them grabbing at me, tearing away at the last shred of humanity I have.

In a last ditch effort, one of my arms swing out and claw at Ravi, digging my thumb into his eye. Blood pools around us as he screams for help, his shriek higher pitched than any girls I used to know.

Hands grip my hair, my skull cracking against the concrete in their last-ditch efforts to subdue me.

Stephan pries my legs open and seats himself between them. If I tighten my thighs, it'll only keep him there, or push him harder against me. Both are outcomes I am not interested in.

He fumbles with his pants as I continue to stare at the ceiling and have my third-world view. If I'm mentally here, it will be my end point. As long as I don't have to be here for it...

"What the fuck was that?" Ravi hisses, head snapping toward me. I don't meet his gaze, instead keeping it upward. His shoe meets my throat, stopping air from entering my lungs. The natural response is to flail around for mercy. My response is remaining utterly still, acting as if it doesn't affect me in any way.

Knowing them both, it only pisses them off until I feel the ground shake slightly.

"Hurricane," I gasp, not even leaving my trained stare. He lifts away from me, a deep snarl engraved on his face. They both get back to work between moving my clothes and undressing themselves before yet another shake is felt. This one is followed by a loud *boom*.

"Get up," Ravi screams, lifting me from the ground and onto his shoulder. His boney shoulder digs into my stomach harshly. I don't complain. The metal on my brace catches on the door causing them to back up and unhook it before moving again. Those seconds were crucial apparently as smoke suddenly swarms around us. They both stop, and Ravi drops me without care.

Falling like a rag doll, their steps are loud as they take off. There's too much pain surrounding every inch of my body to move.

Moving is overrated anyway.

Chapter Twenty-Six

NOMAD

Taking off into the building, we bypass more explosives. It's like a maze with the added incentive to go the right way or have a limb potentially blown off. Several more detonate, forcing us to change route as we storm the building. Smoke starts billowing from inside, streaming through the windows so harshly there's a slight shriek.

Pointing to the side, we band together and wait for the signal. All other units need to be at any point of exit available.

"Move," Crusher commands. One of the prospects was tasked with the battery ram, so rearing back, he slams it into the metal door. The hinges fly off with the force, and even I'm a little surprised with how easily it gave way. That, or this prospect could probably kick my ass.

Glass shatters as the barrier breaks, smoke pouring out of the doorway and through the broken windows. Grabbing the gas masks, we pray that they will work until we can find her. It doesn't take long for us to make our way through the club house as we pretty much memorized the floor plan. If anything, the smoke has helped keep our cover.

Sort of.

Faint coughing brings me out of my thoughts. We can't leave without her. Won't.

"Fuck, turn," a guy calls, running right into us. Without hesitation, Razor grabs the guy and pins him to the ground. Another guy follows behind the first, effectively being grabbed and slammed by another prospect I can't see.

"Subdued," they call, dragging them back outside. According to the infrared, there were three guys. Two just walked right into their own deaths, fucking idiots. The third however...

"Don't move!" We immediately halt, squinting in an attempt to see through the smoke. It's pointless as there's only a silhouette visible. "You move, she dies!" Without being able to see, we can't tell if he's bluffing or not.

"What do you want?" I shout, holding an arm out to stop them from attacking. "You have something of ours. We want her back."

"I had a buyer lined up. You're ruining my chances of profit!" I can't help the rolling in my stomach from his words.

A buyer...

"You were going to sell her?" I retort, doing my best to keep the growl out of my tone. If we set him off, who knows what he'll do.

"She was mine first!" He snaps, the distinctive click of a gun chamber latching into place ricochets around us. "I bought her outright!" The fact that he talks about her like she's an object makes my stomach twist. The burning rage I feel at this man talking about her like this...I want nothing more than to take my fucking side piece and blast his brains through the wall. It doesn't help that it smells like something's starting to burn.

"Look man," I start, choosing my words very carefully. "You won't make that profit if she's dead. I bet she's passed out from the smoke in here. You can't make that money if you don't get her out."

"We're not going anywhere until you're long gone." Movement is seen, but it's hard to figure out what he's doing. It looks as if he's squatting to see if I'm right.

Fuck, she's got smoke lung.

My heart races in my chest at the thought of anything happening to her. If we weren't quick enough...

"We'll go," I digress, hearing a few outraged growls. Using my arm, I start shoving us backwards, praying they'll follow suit.

And they do. No questions asked, they all start to back up. If that's what it takes for her to be alive, that's what we'll do. We can intercept them when he tries to run. If he's also inhaled some heavy smoke, I doubt he's going to be able to run for long with her unconscious weight. When we step out of the house, I immediately start barking orders.

"Eye on exits, they're moving!" We all spread out around the exits and in the tree-line, out of eyesight. A glimpse of red flickers from one of the windows.

"Fire," Razor grunts, getting ready to race inside. Grasping his shoulder tightly, he doesn't move.

"Bird up," I command. With an immediate affirmation, it doesn't take long before another drone is whirling around in the sky above the building.

"Active heat registers in several areas. Zero body registers located. Give me a minute," Techy growls, circling the building a few times. "Negative."

It's like something feral inside of me snaps. This overwhelming protective part of my being that I haven't seen in years.

"If I'm not out in ten, get rescue." Before anyone can respond, I take off into the house once more. I'm able to slip around quieter than before. This time, though, there's embers burning away at the wooden structure. In my head, I use the map to coordinate where I'm going. In an effort to keep from inhaling too much smoke, I crumble my hulking body to the ground in a squat walk. It's painful as all hell, yet it's better than running through clouds.

A voice starts talking over the coms. I can tell it's Techy trying to talk, but the static is making whatever he is saying crackle. My eyes start burning harshly, tears springing and falling down my cheeks.

"If you can hear me, I can't hear you. I'm good for now," I call back, alarm bells ringing in my head as I take another corner. There's something on the floor in front of me, unmoving. Unable to make out what it is, I crouch to a crawl. Thank goodness for gloves. The concrete floor is uneven with lots of shit littering it.

More heaviness weighs down on the smoke above, seeping closer to the ground as it starts puffing faster into the building. Fires broke out before I entered, so the faster we get out, the better.

Finally, like a damn gust of air moving everything around, the thick fog clears for a brief moment. There's a dainty foot lying face up, dried blood cracked on the bottom.

"Found her!" I call into the com, my chest struggling to fully breath. A mix of relief and overwhelming irritation swirl inside me. She's here, but I can't tell if she's alive.

There's blood pooling around her head, the metal fixator that was on her leg is nowhere to be seen. I don't know if something happened, but she'll need that fixed immediately. Trying, and failing, to focus on her chest for air flow, it appears to be completely still.

"Extraction," Techy shouts over the com clearer than before. "Fires...out of there..." The com continues to glitch as I get a quick assessment. Her entire being is disheveled, blood covering the floor around her body. Deciding to take the risk, I heave her over my shoulder and stand to my full height. She doesn't have a mask, but if I can make it back...

A loud bang rattles the room causing me to stumble backward. Aspen's added weight doesn't help my balance. As I look up, a timber comes screaming downward. If it falls in front of me, we'll be trapped. My bleary eyes are struggling to focus.

Taking the risk, I race forward, my knees threatening to give out from the uneven ground and moving foundation from whatever is happening. It cracks on the ground, hot embers flying everywhere and landing on the back of my pants, searing a hole in the material.

I'm sure some landed on my girl. My thoughts falter as my legs move us to safety.

My girl... I've officially claimed her.

"Status?" Crackles Appa, as another rumble heaves the ground.

"Shaky but we're almost back," I respond, my throat tightening from the lack of oxygen. The smokey taste of the air is finally seeping into the mask.

"Left!" He shouts, just as another beam tumbles to the ground. Taking the turn, I can see where most of the smoke is headed toward the open doorway. Damn near tumbles from another ground quake, I manage to trip out of the doorway. Shielding her body with mine, a final *boom* shrieks from the building as pieces of debris go flying.

I brace around her small form, the sounds dying away from around us with a sharp ring in my ears. There's shit flying everywhere, and I'm too scared to move in the event that something decides to fall on us. I need to protect her.

Rough hands grab my shoulders, attempting to move me. An animalistic roar leaves me in an effort to protect the female I rescued.

"We need to get you guys help! Move!" Razor shouts, shoving me back again. My limbs go heavy against his hands. He successfully grabs the girl and takes off, leaving me there to try and collect myself.

The mask is yanked off my face a moment later, Clubby doing a tuck and roll maneuver to hoist me over his shoulders horizontally.

"I can walk," I cough out the lie. We both know damn well I wouldn't be able to make it five steps.

"I'm sure you could, brother. Just here to help," he responds, indulging in my lie. "Also, that was nine minutes and fifty-eight seconds."

The throaty laugh escapes me, pride lightening my heart just a bit. "You kept track?"

"You made an order, we followed it."

Chapter Twenty-Seven

 TECHY

"Is he okay?" I ask, watching as Clubby heaves my husband into the Techy van.

"If you mean pain in my ass, then yeah, he's fine." Rolling his eyes, he gives Nomad a respective jerked nod before going back to the other guys. He tries to sit up, when his eyes cross and he groans.

"Why is the world spinning so damn fast?" He rumbles, his face turning a little green. Appa hands him a plastic bag to heave into. "Fuck, I don't feel good." A moment later, he's throwing up like his life depends on it. Between coughing, sputtering and trying to catch his breath, it's not a pretty sight. Robo looks a little queasy himself but manages to keep it together.

"Take over," I mumble, getting up out of my seat to fully assess him. Doc is currently working on Aspen while Heallie assists. "You okay?" I ask him, grabbing my small flash light and clicking it on. He shakes his head, eyes shut tightly. Most likely to stave off the incessant dizziness. It's probably not making it much better.

"Fuck," he croaks. His throat bobs heavily several times in a row as if he's trying to swallow something too thick. "My throat..." he heaves, doubling over in a coughing fit.

"Can you see if the girls have a spare vac?" Robo is quick to get out of the van, taking the task for himself. Withholding a chuckle, even that seemed to amuse Nomad.

"I'm fine." His voice is anything but fine. There's an unusual strain on his vocals that wasn't there before. Definitely from the smoke. I didn't think it would have affected him this bad, even with the mask on.

I just hope Aspen is okay.

"Alright Wheezy, open up," I command, witnessing him attempt to defy my order. It's not usual for me to boss him around. It's a nice change.

His jaw drops open wide, letting me get a good look at the back of his mouth. He keeps his eyes closed tightly as I drag the light all around. The most I see is swelling and redness, which is pretty usual.

"Is she okay?" He asks mid-inspection.

"Eyes," I state, waiting for him to open those beautiful blues. When they fling open, I cover one with my palm and flash the light into them. His pupils dilate properly, no negative signs.

"Answer my question," he rasps, emotion thick in his tone. "Her fixator wasn't on when I got there, I couldn't see her breathing. I don't even know if she's alive. She can't die-"

"Hey," I call, stopping him from his slow unraveling. It kills me to lie to him, but I can't have him focusing on that right now. "She's fine. Just take a minute to relax." Heaving a breath, he gets thrown into another coughing fit. The van doors bang open and Robo stands there with a vac bag and mask.

"Here ya go." He hands me the vac and bag. "They're loading up to go. One guy is in custody, the other two are still missing.

We've got guys tracking them now. When Aspen wakes up, she'll help us ID them." He helps hook Nomad to the bag, lying him flat on the ground as Appa starts packing the technology equipment with Robo's assistance. I plug it into the generator and it starts automatically pumping oxygen.

"We need to get moving," I tell Nomad, kissing his head. He nods slightly, eyes closing briefly. Smacking his cheek lightly, they snap open with irritation. "You can't go to sleep. Once we finish packing, I'll sit with you."

"Doc called a friend to meet us at the clubhouse to help with Nomad," Appa says, wrapping cords around his arm quickly and tossing them into totes.

Getting to my feet, Nomad struggles to keep himself awake. I can't help the heaviness that weighs down on me for leaving him alone. There's a cord near me that needs to be wrapped, so I grab it and start to furl it when Nomad's eyes start closing again. Dropping the cord on the counter, I smack him again.

"Stay awake," I command with a narrow gaze. He definitely wants to roll his eyes, but I can see that it makes him even more tired.

"You stay with him, we got it," Robo says from the front where he's shutting machines down.

"Thanks man," I mutter, sitting back down. Nomad seems to blink slower and slower, my concern rocketing tenfold. "We should get moving," I announce, doing my best to keep him awake.

"We'll see if we can squeeze him in with Aspen in the med vehicle." Robo races over to the medical van.

"Nomad, you have to stay awake." Smacking him a little hard, he grunts in annoyance but keeps his eyes closed.

"They've got room!" Robo yells across the lot, coming back this way with Clubby, who wastes no time in heaving his loyal brother onto his shoulders. I unhook the oxygen vac, my two prospects agreeing to finish up here.

"What's his status?" Heallie asks, running up to us and following along.

"We've been fighting him to stay awake. Oxygen seemed to just make him more tired." She nods, taking notes and slipping a clip thing over his finger. Looking over, she must notice my overall confusion. "It's an oximeter. I need to get a read on his levels."

A few more paces, and Clubby is setting Nomad into the medic van on the bench. The small device beeps softly causing Heallie to pale.

"We need to get moving. He's at eighty-nine percent." Doc whips around, looking at the ghostly Nomad.

"Hook him to fluids, oxygen mask going. Take manual BP," she calls out, putting her to work. Immediately, she jumps to action. Clubby and I take a step back, letting them do their work no matter how much I want to jump in there and keep him close.

"Why don't you go help the guys? We can't fit anyone else in here," Doc says, smiling softly. I nod, knowing she's right. There's literally nothing I can do.

Taking one step backward, then another, and another before I'm forced to turn on my heel. Palpitations in my heart have my own steps faltering.

I have to be strong. For him. For her. For them.

"We thought you were going with them?" Robo asks, reaching to buckle up.

"They didn't have room. Can one of you take his bike back?" The lump in my throat seems to grow when thinking of someone else handling his baby. He'd hate that someone else is even touching it, let alone riding it.

"Widower already got someone to take it back. We're just waiting for final confirmation to go," Appa confirms with a tight smile. "We almost left your ass."

"I would've made you hack the craziest thing. I'll give you a Vernam cypher. It would drive you nuts," I retort. They know damn well that I could make them insane with a fucking riddle on the mega walls. Appa looks like he's about to get out, where I stop him and offer to get into the back. They protest quietly. Rolling my eyes, I get in and their objections quiet. Soft music fills the speakers as the convoy starts rolling.

Thoughts of what could be going on in the medical van haunt me slightly. All potential outcomes floor my brain. Doc and Heallie were both oddly troubled by whatever the reader said. I'm tempted to pull out my phone and search what it meant, but I decide against it. People diagnose themselves with cancer all the time because of the internet, so I don't want to be one of those individuals.

Thinking about it, I didn't even look at Aspen. My heart was racing and cracking all at the same time from the thought of my husband dying on me.

Why wasn't I more concerned? I obviously think of her consistently, she's one of the main thoughts that swirl my brain along with my husband. Yet, when she was an arms length away...

"Stop it," I hiss, my hands finding their way into my hair and tugging harshly.

"You good?" Appa asks, looking in the rearview. I keep my hands in my hair, head down. "Boss?" Releasing a heavy sigh, my world feels like it's coming off the axis.

"Yeah," I mutter, dropping my hands and letting my head hang. "I'm alright."

"If you need to talk," Appa starts, hesitation clear in his tone. With a shake of my head, I let it go. The van jerks around the road, probably sliding on ice as we go. Peeking from the window, there's heavy snowfall coming from the sky. Sides of the roads that were previously slushed with dirt are now starting to turn white again. The road crew will have a fun time trying to get the salt layed out for the traffic tomorrow.

"We're here." Jumping out of the van, I don't wait for them. They're plenty capable enough to get the shit sorted. It's like my own personal race to get down to the medical wing. He can't be alone, he needs to know I'm here. She does too. They both need me, and to know that I'm not going anywhere.

Unfortunately, I'm stopped before I can even open the damn doors.

"Doc asked me to stave you off," Hudson says, stepping in front of the doors. A low growl releases from deep within my stomach, one that I didn't even realize I was capable of making.

"Move," I rumble. If it wasn't Widower's husband and co-prez, I would have shoulder-checked him on my way through. I may not be the biggest guy, but my husband is lying on his fucking death bed for all I know.

Deep fucking breath.

"Go help the guys," he orders with a jerked nod. It takes everything in me to swallow the growl. Turning on my heel, I fume and push myself to keep going. If I stop for even a second, I'll throw myself through that door to get to them.

Chapter Twenty-Eight

 *Aspen*

I swear to all above...my body feels like I got run over by a ten ton truck. *Again.*

Trying, and failing, to open my eyes, I listen to the noises around me. They're all a little overwhelming. A pitch of white noise is shrouding the background while people talk. There's an incessant beeping that seems to be getting harsher. Closer and closer, louder and louder, I can't seem to escape the chaos in my brain. My throat aches with the need to simply scream in frustration. It feels as though weights are placed on my arms and legs, stopping me from even making a single movement.

Large lumps are stuck in my throat as I attempt to swallow past them. Except with each pass, there's a hint of smokiness pluming in my mouth. It's not like when you eat smoked meat. No, this is a burning sensation that over-stimulates your senses.

So much so, that my body finally takes notice we're alive and throws us into a celebratory coughing fit.

"She's fine," someone calls, causing a lot of commotion to seize as my lungs feel like they're going to give out. If I opened my eyes right this moment, I could guarantee there's a layer of dust on the sheets from how much I'm releasing.

"Come on, pretty girl. Breathe," a rumbling voice demands. The way my body responds to him is unlike anything I'd ever experienced before. Sucking in deep lungfuls of air, my brain finally clears. "That's a good girl." Goosebumps break out across my skin at the praise, a wracked shiver pinging down my spine.

My jaw finally seems to slacken from its tight confines, opening slowly to try and tell them to kick rocks.

Nothing seems to come out even as I force it, only garbled air. The bed is slowly pushed up into a sitting position, my eyes still tightly sealed against my will.

"Open those pretty eyes for me," another melodic voice lilts. Like fucking magic, the muscles loosen and allow me to slowly blink.

"Shit," I raspily hiss. The bright lights around us are on full blast, staring right down onto my wounded body. The melodic voice curses slightly, and the heat from the lights lessens as they're turned down.

"Try again." And I do. This time, they're softer. Two brazen men stand on either side of my bed. They're both too handsome for their own good. The bearded male brings a cup and straw to my face, letting me take slow sips of water. He pulls away slowly, his movements leisurely.

Brows furrowed in confusion, I flit between the two men.

"Who are you?" I ask, my voice feeling like fucking sandpaper in my throat. It's as if they're both shocked to the core, Doc also appearing confused.

My shoulders start shaking before the rest of me. A laugh bursts from my lips, the freedom in my soul seemingly carrying into this new chapter.

They saved me. Just like I knew they would.

Did I have any doubts? Only for a few moments, before I realized that Techy and Nomad both pinky swore that they'd keep me safe. They even sealed it with a knuckle kiss.

"Oh, you little," Nomad growls playfully, narrowing his beautiful blues on me. Turning to Techy, his gray eyes are also filled with a mix of humor and irritation. I don't think I could forget them even if I tried.

"I'm glad to see you feeling better," Doc says, standing at the foot of the bed. I chuff a mirthless laugh.

"That's a stretch. I feel like I'm grandma from that one song. The one who got slammed by Santa with his reindeer?" I cackle, the smokiness not quite clearing from my throat.

"Tis' the season," she nods with a sweet smile. Turning to gaze out the window, there's significant amounts of snow falling to the ground. A thick layer sits on the window sill while the rest of it falls. "You were out a couple days, nothing drastic. It's completely normal for smoke inhalation. I need to run a few tests, keep you for a couple extra days for observation. Then, if all is clear, you'll be free to go." An uncontrolled groan leaves me at the thought of staying in the hospital. Last time I was in the hospital, I was told my leg was all sorts of fucked up.

Looking down, there's no fixator. There's a few pieces of white bandage over where the holes were but nothing else.

"It was removed before you got here," she informs me, nodding once. Taking a moment to wrack my brain, nothing pops up as to when it was removed.

"How could it get removed without opening the skin?"

"Actually, this one I could manually remove from the exterior. Honestly, I think you'll be good with some therapy and a hinged ROM brace."

"A what?" I urge, my brain failing to catch all of the details being thrown my way.

"ROM? Range of motion." She pulls back the blanket slightly, and there's a metal brace already there. "It has hinges on the side to stop your leg from bending too far backward. As you get through therapy, you'll be able to do more."

"How long is therapy?" Nomad asks, bringing my knuckles to his lips for a gentle kiss.

"Anywhere from six weeks to twelve weeks, if not more. You'll just be working with Heallie." The girl in question waves from the corner. That just shows my observation skills.

"What about extracurriculars?" I ask, feeling a blush take form on my chest. The heat creeps up my neck all the way to my ears. Ignoring the questioning glances from the men, Doc nods enthusiastically.

"No kneeling or using the leg at all," she begins, looking down at her chart. I'd only be able to lay on my back or side, but I think that could work.

"Easy enough." Smiling, Heallie and Doc go through the motions of taking vitals, drawing blood, and giving more fluids. She has the boys leave while she removes the catheter.

"Are you thinking about having intercourse with them?" She questions quietly, no judgment evident in her tone.

"I think so," I whisper, tears springing into my eyes. "I feel like I need to take myself back. Give myself the love I deserve." She smiles knowingly, nodding her head.

"Those two seem to be head over heels for you. When we brought you and Nomad in, it was chaotic. We got you both settled and stable without complications. He woke up, ripped out of his stuff and demanded to know how you were. It was like the fucking hulk had taken over his body," she laughs. I can't help giggling along with her, knowing that seems to be an appropriate response for him.

"What about Techy?" She finishes her paperwork and slips the clipboard back into the tray at the foot of the bed.

"He just about clobbered Hudson, according to the man himself. I requested he wait in case something happened to you or Nomad. Thankfully it didn't, but we can't be too careful." I nod knowingly. "Either way, Hudson turned him around, but Techy wasn't too happy. Once he heard Nomad was awake, there was no stopping him." Another giddy laugh bubbles from me at the thought of Techy tearing down the world for Nomad.

Those two give me hope in the future.

One that I've been hoping to see them in since the very beginning. Nothing but amazing men, they're both extremely protective. Do I feel bad for scaring them earlier? A little bit. Okay, maybe not at all. The point is, I saw their concern. The crushed look they both had was almost soul crushing for me. At first, it was a deer in the headlights.

"You're safe with them," she reassures, patting my arm gently. "Just remember that you're not on birth control, so you'll need protection."

"Oh." Exhaling sharply, the biggest disappointment of my life is about to be revealed. "Actually...the guys before I came here. They...uhm," I struggle to even breathe right now. That thick ball returns to the center of my wind-pipe, crushing me from the inside out.

"Whatever it is, I can guarantee they'll be more than under-standing," she implores, sitting down in the rolling chair. Heallie takes that cue to leave, softly shutting the door behind her.

I can't meet Doc's eye. There's going to be judgment, disappointment.

"I can't have babies," I whisper, the painful sting of tears hitting the backs of my eyes. If I looked up, I'd see the look of rejection from her face. Except when I do tilt to look at her, she's gone. Replaced with the two men in question.

Chapter Twenty-Nine

Aspen

My own worst nightmare has doubled in terror. How fun. They're both stock still, expressions hardened and stoic. A silent sob wracks my body. The echoing sound seems to bring them out of their stupor, rushing toward me on either side. Like a dam breaking, tears freely flow down my cheeks. Taking my hands in theirs, they switch between whispering words of assurance, rubbing my hair, and kissing my knuckles.

"We'll get you some testing and labs, just in case, baby girl." There's a deep passion lilted in Nomad's voice, one that burns fiercely. "Even if that's the case, you don't need to be afraid. If you want kids in the future, we can look into other options."

"You think an adoption agency will adopt to us?" I cry, shoulders wracking harder as the tears flow faster. Everything I'd been holding in seems to break away. Despair and dejection fill my heart as I think about the inability.

I'd always wanted to be a mother, wanted to have those experiences. Then I'm sold and shipped all over the world before landing with my three captores. They didn't want to wrap up, so...they took it upon themselves to deal with it.

I was given a hysterectomy without my consent. There's scars lining my stomach where they poked holes and suture marks to tie it together. My fate was sealed by those stitches.

My head is grasped between two strong hands, forcing me to look up at Nomad. His own eyes are watery, cheeks still dry. A visible lump is stuck in his own throat as he works to clear it out. After a few moments of staring at one another, he slowly leans in, brushing our noses together.

"I want to kiss you so badly," he whispers, nuzzling my face with his. I can't help the smile that takes over my lips. The clouds finally seem to move away, allowing sunshine to pour through the darkness that shrouds my heart.

"Nothing is stopping you," I rasp in return, the smoke in my throat still working to clear itself. Whatever hesitation that shimmered in his eyes is now gone, replaced by a gentle need. One that I'll admit I'm not familiar with.

Pulling away from me, he assesses my face fully. His own ocean blue eyes seem to draw me into their current. Wave after wave crashes through his gaze as he drinks me in.

"Are you sure?" He doesn't allow me to look away from the intenseness of his stare. It's more than just waves. It's a full blown tsunami ready to tear through the world on my behalf.

"This is the most sure I've been about anything in a long time," I mutter. Fully expecting him to crash his lips against mine, I brace for the impact.

Other than...it doesn't come.

Instead, he slowly brings those plush cushions to drag over my cold lips. Eyes fluttering closed, he takes his time with me. There's a sweetness behind his kiss that's clearly intentional. It's at odds with his rough exterior.

Not that I'm complaining.

His tongue flicks my bottom lip, pushing my two apart to allow him in. Stars dance behind my eyelids, my brain turning foggy as he takes his time with me. The kiss feels meant to be, like I've waited my whole life just to be with him.

After what feels like an eternity, he pulls away slowly. His pupils are blown wide, the blacks nearly taking over the beautiful blue. He looks blissed out simply from a kiss. It's a true vision, seeing him so worked up over something so small.

My core clenches with a need that I presumed was dead after the trauma I've endured. A fire ignites inside of me, flames licking my body as a renewed sense of belonging takes place.

I'm going to take back my life. Everything that was unwillingly taken from me, I'm going to bring it back to life. It's going to be better than it was before, that's for fucking sure.

"You're a fucking Cobra," Techy mutters, grabbing my chin softly and turning me towards him. With his own heartfelt kiss, he devours me. Without words, he affirms that everything is going to be okay. They're going to make it better, one small step at a time.

Emotions pour from him straight into me, almost as if he's filling my cup with love.

Love. That's an emotion I've not felt since the day I was sold to trafficking for my parents to make a quick buck. For a few seconds, I debate if that's what I'm really feeling. Maybe it's something else like adoration or a sense of companionship. As waves of serenity fill my emptiness, I realize that it's them. They're filling me full of something I'd long forgotten.

It's several long moments before Techy finally retreats, pressing his forehead against mine. Our breath match is beat as we attempt to catch them.

"We talked with Widower. We'd like to find you a spot in the clubhouse, if you're willing." Sitting frozen, my limbs zing to life. Initiating me as part of the club...

They must see the look on my face. "You'd be similar to what Maggie is, an honorary member. There are things we wouldn't be able to share with you, but you'll be part of the crew."

"Do I get to learn to ride?" I ask, a thundering heat spearing through Nomad.

"If you mean by riding on the back of my bike, then yes." I can hear the sarcasm dripping from his lips as he licks them. It takes everything in me not to roll my eyes at him.

"I mean learn to drive one, ding-dong," I sass, moving to sit up a little more. Heaviness weighs down on my body, and the two men jump into action. They help me settle back in for a long night. Just as I open my mouth, my leg shoots burning pains up and into the rest of me. Groaning, I shut my eyes tightly.

"We'll get Doc in here with some meds." Techy shoots out of his chair, making haste out of the room. A small giggle escapes me as I think about everything they've done for me so far. The protection, the vulnerability. All of it. They've been my rock since we met. Even at my worst, they wanted me to be my best. Pushed me to get better without forcing me into it.

"Thank you," I sigh, reaching out for him. His large hand encapsulates my smaller one. Warmth radiates from his palm as he draws slow circles on the back of my hand.

"You know we'd do just about anything for you," he vows, leaning forward and brushing a gentle kiss on my forehead. "I'm sorry we weren't able to be there sooner, pretty girl. There was a lot going on, then trying to track you down and get everything together-" Darting my hand out, it meets the back of his neck and yanks him toward me. A grunt mixed with a groan purrs from his chest as his lips slant over mine once more.

It's like an electrical current zaps through me. I feel rejuvenated. Alive. Free.

I feel free.

Pulling away, more tears spring into my eyes. "Don't apologize. I had so much hope..." I smile, shaking my head like an overly emotional idiot. "There was a small part of my brain that was sure I'd never see you guys again, that I'd be trapped right where I started. Then, there was a larger voice in my heart and gut that both agreed you'd be back to save me.

It's cliche, the damsel in distress. Yet, there's something mystifying about how they were able to find me.

"I hear a special patient is hurting?" Doc teases as she enters the room, Techy hot on her heels.

"Yeah, I feel kind of crampy." She nods knowingly. Walking over to the IV, she checks everything before turning to the pharmacy cabinet. Swiping her card, the locker opens. After a moment, she grabs a small vile and needles, dragging out the liquid into the syringe and pushing it into my tubing.

"This will make you drowsy. You have a couple minutes left before you'll knock out," she informs with a small smile. Disposing of everything, she double checks that everything is good before exiting quietly.

It doesn't even take a minute before there's a lightness in my head from the medication. Ah, the good shit. Well, it's good when it's not forced on you.

"Get some rest," Nomad sighs, kissing my knuckles. A sleepy grin showcases my teeth as I work to keep my eyes from drooping.

"You're going to need it, little Cobra," Techy mutters, his lips landing on my temple softly.

"I love you guys," I mumble, my eyes drifting shut as my mind finally falls silent long enough for me to sleep.

Chapter Thirty

NOMAD

We both freeze in our places.

"Did she just..." he trails off, shock enveloping his features. The sleeping beauty laying before us just gave us the ultimate shock of our lives.

"Yeah," I huff a laugh, shaking my head as a beaming smile breaks out across my face. Happiness radiates from me at her small confession. Did she mean it? Hopefully. She's pretty out of it if she's slipping secrets, but I can't help the happy palpitations my heart is doing. At my laugh, Techy's head whips up to look at me. His own expression is one that I can't really read. If anything, there's a smidge of self-deprecation. Destruction.

My smile drops as tears pool in his gray eyes, swirling around and basking in utter sadness.

"What's going on?" Standing from my chair, I make my way toward him. He can't seem to make the words come out of his mouth, instead releasing a heart shattering sob. If I wasn't sure Aspen was knocked out by the medications, I would be absolute that the sounds would wake her.

"I don't deserve her." His bulky shoulders tremble as our bodies collide. Unfortunately, this isn't completely uncommon. My wonderful, sexy husband doesn't seem to know his worth. Planting my lips over him, I kiss the life back into him.

I'll teach him over and over again, even if it doesn't stick. His trust stems from his own background, which I can understand in its entirety, but I'll be the rock he needs. Forever and always. Just like we vowed on our wedding day three years ago...

My hands tremble. Waiting at the altar, I feel like tearing my hair out. I can't believe a few other guys did this before me. I'm about ready to piss myself in anticipation.

A strong hand claps my shoulder, shaking me from my stupor. Hudson smiles knowingly toward the closed doors at the end of the aisle, a smirk casting on his mouth.

"Amelia said he's just about as nervous as you are," he laughs quietly, coming to adjust my tie. I want to swat him away but don't. He's doing his due diligence as my best man.

"Good to know I'm not the only one losing my mind," I snort. Shaking out my hands, he finishes re-doing the long tie into a simpler knot. "I don't know why I'm so fucking nervous. It's not like I'm marrying some stranger."

"Cut yourself some slack, big guy. Mine and your Prez's marriage was technically arranged, and I was about to blow my load just thinking about her back then." I cackle at his crude words, remembering how he did look antsy at the altar.

"I've got to get out there to do the walk of honor." Clapping my shoulder, he double checks my attire to make sure I'm all good. Paired in my signature jeans, they put me in a dark navy blue blazer with a light blue button up and tie. They wouldn't let me wear my cut,

but did compromise on letting me wear jeans instead of slacks. They even made me put gel in my beard to keep it from being too awry. My hair was trimmed and is slicked back, giving me a posher look than I'm used to, Does it look weird? Probably. Do I care? Definitely not.

He slips through the crack in the door, a laugh ringing before they're quietly shut again. Sweat beads on my forehead in anticipation. I have zero clue what he'd be wearing. Women usually wear dresses, but what would a guy wear when in the position of the bride?

Music suddenly starts on the baby grand piano that Pax insisted we have. The notes start off strong to a song that I've not heard in years. The song that I first ever heard him play on the piano. Overwhelmed, a sole tear slips down my cheek. Moonbeams *by Barbara Arens echoes around the small area. The doors open to Hudson and Widower stepping out, walking slowly toward me with beaming smiles on their faces. They look exactly how I feel. As they reach me, they both have tears welling in their eyes, faces flushed with excitement.*

"Congratulations," Widower whispers, kissing my cheeks and standing where Pax will soon. Crusher and Maggie follow behind them, giving their love to us. A few more people come through that I'm not too familiar with, but Pax must know them as they give us their best wishes and praises.

Finally, after what feels like ages, there's a change in song. I can't help the laugh that slips from my lips. Of course it's a song from one of his favorite musicals. All I Ask of You *from Phantom of the Opera starts.*

The doors cast open, and in walks the love of my life.

He's wearing a matching button-up shirt covered by an off-white blazer. He's wearing a bow tie to contrast mine. Dark navy slacks to match my blazer, he's wearing oxford shoes as his flare of nerd. At least, that's what I'm going with.

There's a beaming light behind him, almost like an angelic glow casting to shine on him. He was definitely sent to save my life. And I'll say, he's done exactly that. Even during the lowest of lows, he's kept me sane.

Crusher takes his place on the altar behind me as Pax finally takes the two steps. Coming face to face, it takes everything inside of me to stop from smashing my lips to his. I want to claim him for everyone to see. Fucking exhibitionist, I know.

"Please be seated," Crusher calls, holding a small notebook as one hand raises. The crowd quiets, sitting down to watch the ceremony. As Crusher starts talking, the world fades. Only Pax exists at this moment.

"At this time, the two grooms will share their vows," Crusher announces, taking a step away from the microphone and turning it toward us. "If you'll go first, Nomad," he says, looking at me. Nodding, I grab the small paper from the pocket inside my jacket.

"Paxton Williams, soon-to-be Bradley, you've made my life worth living. Before you, my heart felt cold, black as coal. It wasn't one that I wanted to be part of. Then you stumbled into my life and seduced me with the wicked grays." The crowd chuckles along as Pax wipes happy tears away. "I vow to always protect you from harm, to stand with you against your troubles, and to look to you when I need protection. You make me laugh, you make me think, and above all, you make me happy.

"I promise to be your navigator, best friend, and husband. I promise to honor, love, and cherish you through all life's adventures. Wherever we go, we'll go together. Your love gives me hope. Your smile gives me joy. You make me a better man." A quiet sob leaves him as a handkerchief is pushing toward him. Camera shutters click as the photographer takes all sorts of angles. I'm sure we'll both look like a m ess.

"And now, Techy," he announces as several sniffles resound.

"How the hell am I supposed to follow that?" He cries out, arms flailing dramatically.

"You'll do just fine," I reassure, grabbing one of his hands and bringing it to my lips. His face flushes a cherry red as the crowd laughs.

"Gosh, what would I do without you?" He sighs. Squeezing my hand, tears start rolling with abandon. *"Today I join my life to yours, not simply as your husband, but as your friend, your lover, and your biggest supporter. Let me be the shoulder you lean on and the companion of your life. You have taught me that two people joined together with respect, trust, and open communication can be far stronger and happier than each could ever be alone. You are the strength I didn't know I needed and the joy that I didn't know I lacked. Today, I choose to spend the rest of my life with you.*

"I promise to love you for who you are, and for who you are yet to become. I promise to be patient and to remember that all things between us are rooted in love. I promise to nurture your dreams and help you reach them. I promise to share my whole heart with you and to remember to show you how deeply I care for you, no matter the challenges that may come our way. I promise to love you loyally and fiercely—as long as I shall live."

"Paxton Williams, do you take Andrew Bradley to be your law-fully wedded husband? In sickness, and in health. For richer and poorer. Till death do you part?"

"I do, forever and always." His ring slips over my finger shakily.

"Andrew Bradley, do you take Paxton Williams to be your law-fully wedded husband? In sickness, and in health. For richer and poorer. Till death do you part?"

"I do," I confirm, sliding my ring onto his finger. "Forever and always."

"By the power vested in me by the State of Washington, I now pronounce you husband and husband." Without waiting another moment, I grasp the back of his neck and smash our lips together. It's just him and I, joining in union for the rest of our lives.

"I love you, Paxton Bradley," I whisper, pulling back from him. Tears swell in his eyes as we stare at one another.

"I love you, Andrew Bradley." His response is low, filled with sorrow and love.

"I'm going to show you just how much you fucking mean to me. But first, I'm going to punish you for even doubting that my love for you is less than."

Chapter Thirty-One

 TECHY

An overly familiar darkness creeps into my heart. There's a layer of black that threatens to take over. If it weren't for my husband...I don't know where I'd be.

In a surprise move for both of us, I launch myself into his arms. He doesn't hesitate to grab me under my thighs and hoists my legs around his waist. Our mouths mold together into one, tongues clashing as he walks us out of Aspen's room.

Once she's awake and able to talk a bit more, we'll introduce her to our lives. Thankfully, neither Nomad nor I need bondage or harmful play to get turned on, but it's definitely a lot more fun.

"Fuck, you're so hot," he rasps against my mouth. Dropping my hips just a smidge, his cock rubs against mine in my jeans. Both of us are rock hard, too wound up from the adrenaline for the past few days. Strike that, the last fucking month has been too much.

Before I can pull back to breathe, he's taking the stairs up to our bedroom. It's more secluded in the corner, further of a walk, the louder I can scream.

This man deserves to be worshiped.

Taking that into consideration, just as he steps over the threshold of our room, I wiggle harshly. He groans a guttural sound at the back of his throat before complying, my legs dropping heavily onto the plush carpet of our room. No warning needed, I drop to my knees. His brows shoot up his forehead before a wicked grin registers over his face. My own gleam in return as I work to undo the buckle.

Large hands encompass my wrists, halting me. "Did I say you could have a taste of me?" He asks, his tone low and husky with need.

"No sir." Batting my lashes at the bulking male, the obvious tent in his jeans makes my mouth water. If I could blink and make his clothes be gone, I absolutely would.

"I want you naked by the time my belt comes off," he yields, taking a single step backward. "Now." The command jolts my bones. Launching back to my feet, he takes his time as I jerk around with serious speed just to do as I'm asked.

Naked in record time, I stand breathless. The belt comes through the last loop as I pant for air.

"Good boy," he coos, looping the belt back into itself and making them into cuffs. "Wrists." Mindlessly, my wrists push outward to him. Lord have mercy. Fastening the loops tightly, he has me wiggle them around to ensure blood flow is still good.

"On the bed, on your back. Head hanging over the edge," he barks. Like a zap, I jump to follow the order. Scrambling, I work myself on the bed and do as asked. "What a good boy you are. Obeying orders is very good. You'll get a good treat after your punishment."

I don't say a damn thing. If you speak out of turn, that could add to the tally of punishments. Instead, I lie there obediently silent.

"Open," he grunts, notching his swollen cock at my mouth. No warning is given as he drives straight to the back. Thankfully, my tongue blocks the gag reflex as he drives in over and over again. My attention is captivated by the man whose balls are slapping my forehead. If my hands weren't tied, I'd be massaging them, maybe even playing with the spot right behind them.

Between the sounds of my slurping and his grunts, my own cock practically doubles in size. My fingers clasp together tightly to stop me from reaching down and bringing myself to orgasm with him. This is my punishment, and I'm sure I'll be getting a flogger to the back when he's done.

"Shit, suck harder," he demands, ramming in and retreating before repeating the process. Again, I follow orders. Hollowing my cheeks, I open my throat completely and breath through my nose as he propels forward. "Yes, yes, yes!" He roars, hot seed coating the back of my throat as he pulses in my mouth. His length jumps and pulsates as he continues to shout praises, cooing at me for sucking him just how he likes it.

Moving backward, he leans down and slants his lips over mine, not caring if his taste still plays in my mouth. His fingers dance in the back of my hair, using it as leverage to hold me steady. Then, he unlatches himself and pushes me upward, forcing my face to plant into the bed with my ass in the air.

"When I'm done with you, there will be no doubt how much you mean to me. Do you understand?" My stomach clenches with unadulterated need. If it weren't so serious, I'd be more of a brat. Except, when I look over my shoulder, I'm not met with the expression of an angry man. No, I'm met with my husband who loves me more than the air he breathes. There's a twinkle in his eye even as he raises his brow in question.

"I understand," I shudder, eyes fluttering shut as his hands roam my ass and back. They spread my ass cheeks but don't move toward the forbidden spot.

"Good. Now, you tell me which one you want." Two things drop next to my body. They're hard to see from the angle, but I can tell they're both whips. It looks like one is a cat-o-nines while the other is a basic flogger.

"Cat," I whine, straining to see behind me again. The two items are removed from my sight and the bed dips behind me. Drew's hard length presses between my ass, but not quite how I'd like it. He simply leaves himself nestled between them while his hands meander over my backside.

"You're too good for me," he mutters, leaning over my body to kiss the back of my throat. Goosebumps break out as his beard grazes my sensitive flesh. I want to shout at him that he's a fool, an idiot to think that I'm any better than he is.

"We are perfect for each other," I retort, pushing backward against his hard body. A quick smack lands on my right ass cheek, followed by a soothing rub.

"Did I say you could speak?" He asks as another painful strike lands on my left side.

"I didn't want you lying to yourself," I nag, the bratty side in me finally showing. It's hard to keep it restrained, especially when I want him to know the honest truth. We're meant to be together because we understand the traumas. There's no hiding it from each other, that's for damn sure.

"You're the best damn thing that ever happened to me," he rasps, his tone thick with emotion. "I would say that the holiday season is the reason for my state, but I also know that my husband is everything I could ever ask for. And then some."

"Please let me look at you," I beg. He sends another quick succession of smacks to my ass, jolts and soothing following one another.

"Punishment first, love making after," he agrees as he reaches for the leather whip. "You're going to count to ten with me. If you stop, we start again. While you count, you're going to tell me just how much we deserve each other. Do you understand me?"

"Yes sir," I croak, my brain working overtime to try and think of ten reasons why we belong together. I just know that this man is my entire being.

The balled ends snap on different areas of my skin, a hiss pouring between my teeth as pleasure quickly follows.

"One," I gasp, my eyes working to uncross themselves from the lovely feeling.

"You forget something?" He snaps as his other hand digs into my hip.

"We belong together because your soul calls to mine," I rasp, balling my fists into the sheets beneath me. Another swift *snap* hits my sensitive skin.

"Two," I whimper, biting my lip as the feeling of sharpness fades. "We belong together because you match my humor fully."

Smack.

"Three! We belong together because you make my heart happy," I pant, the sore flesh of my ass and back starting to burn.

Smack.

"Four! We belong together because you're my reason for breathing." Then, the last six come in rapid succession. I don't have the mental capacity to count as they hit, but I do count all the way to ten once my brain registers.

"We belong together because my life would be utterly useless without you in it," he croaks. Whatever thin string snaps inside of me as I rip the belt off my hands without a care for the chafe.

I spin around and narrow him with my gaze. Fingers tangling in the ends, I slam his lips to mine in a passionate, soul bleeding kiss. Everything I want to say and need to tell him all comes pouring out. From my soul to his.

"You're my everything," I mumble against his lips. Our cocks stroke together as he rolls his hips.

"I don't know where I would be without you," he gasps, pulling away from me briefly. Unshed tears fill his eyes as I realize the gravity of the situation. My own darkness blanketed me from his pains. I thought I was in tune with him when in reality I was letting him drown.

"I'm sorry I've not been there for you," I sigh. He leans his forehead against mine as he shakes it. "With everything going on, we've not gotten the chance to reconnect."

"Let's take that opportunity now, then." Putting weight on my body, we go tumbling backward into the bed. Most of his mass is on his arms, but his naked cock meets mine. Reaching to the bedside table, he grabs the lube and situates it next to us after he drops some onto his fingers. His large frame forces me open, but his other hand traces softly between my thighs. It's a soft feeling, one that would confuse a virgin if they'd never been with this brute before.

Warm, wet fingers rub at my puckered back hole before one pushes inward. The muscles contract around the knuckle as he continues inward. I try to breathe through it, but a groan of satisfaction leaks from my sealed lips.

"You're so fucking sexy," he growls. Lips latch around my nipple as his teeth nibble. Contrasting feelings cause my toes to curl. Then he hits *that* spot.

I damn near come off the bed. "Fuck yes," I drag out, eyes rolling toward the back of my head. He chuckles and crooks his finger in a come-hither motion.

"I'm going to cum if you don't stop," I warn, my voice an octave or two higher than normal. The bearded hulk simply smirks, adding another finger. He doesn't touch my sweet spot again. Instead, he focuses more on ensuring his monster cock will fit inside of me.

Grabbing the lube again, he squirts a massive amount and uses his fist to fuck it around himself. The image is surreal, and if I could get wet, I'd be fucking soaked. Since I can, my cock decides to jump for joy and wait for his turn to be touched.

"You ready?" He asks, notching himself at my entrance. Words escape my brain where I can only nod. Usually, he'd demand for me to speak. This time, he lets it slide. Fisting himself at the base, his swollen head pushes inside my tight heat. I fight my eyes to stay open, the sensation on the edge of too-painful as my ass works to adjust to his girth.

His bulbous head finally pops inside, the ring of muscle spasming slightly as he continues to push.

"Fuck, you're too tight." He exhales loudly and doesn't stop moving as he rolls his hips forward until our pelvises are flush together. "Shit, Pax. You're such a good boy."

"Fuck me," I whimper, my fingers tightly gripping the sheets in an effort to stay grounded in this moment. I want nothing more than to let my brain fly away into the highest of highs. But I don't. I stay right here with him.

"Your wish is my command." Retracting slowly, he slams forward harshly. Air whooshes out of my lungs with the impact. Again, he moves oh-so-slowly until only the tip is there, then sinks into me with abandon. A wanton cry rips from me, and it's like the chains have been snapped.

One leg is tossed over his shoulder while the other is spread out straight. Thrusting frantically, he wraps his lube covered hand around my own cock. He uses a corkscrew method to add a bit of friction.

I'm fucking done for.

"Oh fuck!" I shriek. My balls draw up into my body and ropes of warm cum shoot from my cock. "I fucking love you!" Drew doesn't let up as he continues to pound into my tight ass.

"I fucking love you," he grunts, his eyes fixated on the never ending orgasm that spills from me.

After what feels like minutes, his movements become jerky and his pace gets uneven as he roars his own release. It's weird to think that some people can feel others orgasming. The most I feel is his cock getting ram-rod hard before he buries himself all the way to the hilt. Can't forget when he cums. It's almost like a wild animal coming unglued.

Several moments pass by before his weight lands right on me. Some people may be uncomfortable with it, but I like it. It's like a heavy weight blanket that adds another level of comfort.

"Are you going to doubt me again?" He asks while nibbling my ear.

"No sir," I sass. We both know I sure as fuck will.

"Tomorrow, we'll ensure that Aspen is on the right track. Then, we'll bring her here and set our intentions straight."

"Sounds like a perfect plan," I whisper. Our lips meet for another heart stopping kiss. His cock had gone soft for a split second, but I can feel him starting to inflate once again.

"Round two?"

Chapter Thirty-Two

 Aspen

Waking up in an unfamiliar room could send alarm bells ringing in my head. That is, if I didn't know two hulking men that had me discharged and taken to their bedroom for 'closer observation'. By that, it meant that they could sleep in the same room as me. Last night, however, I had to sleep in a different room due to some cleaning or something. They had to stay at a hotel last night since there weren't enough rooms, and they didn't want me to go out of the club's safety.

I continue to think about how they never forget about me or my safety. Even if it means sleeping in the same room as them. While I'm not quite comfortable sleeping in the same bed as them, they're both extremely understanding. When I woke up the first night in there, I was shocked to see another bed on the other side of the room. When I asked, they said that they wanted to make sure I was safe while also respecting my wishes. I'm still not sure whether I want to slap them or kiss them.

Who am I kidding? I definitely want to kiss them both. Maybe even at the same time?

Shaking the dirty thoughts from my head, I'm astonished to feel my core getting tight and clenching with need. After being in captivity most of my teens and adulthood, I forgot what good sex was. All I know is...

My shoulders shudder with the terrifying thought. I refuse to bring that piece back into my life. Doc and I continue to work through it, and I honestly feel like I'm ready for the next step.

Exposure therapy.

This time, though, it's not going to be jumping into the deep end. Doc and I have been talking about it for about a week now, and we both agreed that I'm ready for the next step with them. While it may not be sex, it's pretty damn close.

What do people call them? Bases?

I want to go to second or third base with them. If all goes well, I may be willing to do a homerun.

The tingly feeling in my core doesn't stop as the two men continue to plague my mind. Looking around me, I double check to make sure I'm all by myself before slipping my fingers into my panties. It's a sensation I'm not familiar with, but as I circle the sensitive bud, my eyes flutter closed.

One set of blues and a set of grays play behind my lids. Wicked smirks gleam back at me as my quiet moans fill the room. I can't hear anything, but I imagine Nomad eating my pussy like a starved man while Techy pounds my mouth with his huge cock. Maybe one of them has a piercing? With a sigh, I rim my entrance before dipping a finger inside. A girl can dream.

My hole contracts around my single finger, fluttering with pleasure instead of pain. Another unfamiliar feeling to add to the list.

"Please," I whisper to nobody in particular, letting the air in my room catch the plea. Using the palm of my hand, I rub my clit hard as another finger is added to the mix. My juices are slowly starting to creep onto my hand, and I use that to push them inside of me faster and faster.

"Oh shit," I gasp, just about to detonate.

The door to my room slams open, causing me to jump ten feet in the fucking air. Techy blushes deeply at the realization that he caught my hand in my pants. Any normal human would hide and scream, but something in his gaze keeps my hand exactly where it's at. Since I stopped, my orgasm receded into itself.

I'll just have to get it back.

My palm digs against my clit once again. I can't help the gasp that sounds from the feeling itself. Deciding to keep eye contact, neither of us move as I continue to work myself back toward that beautiful edge.

"Yes," I rasp, hooded lids threatening to shut completely. A shadow looms behind Techy as his hulking husband steps into the room. Once he realizes what's happening, he shuts the door softly and locks it. Striding up to me, he jerks back the covers and finds me fingering myself into oblivion.

I don't know what's come over me, but I'm not about to back down now.

"You want help?" He purrs from above me, reaching behind himself and yanking his shirt over his head. Bare chested and glistening with sweat, I fight the urge to sit up and lick his taut body. Nomad's deep growl seems to snap Techy out of whatever stupor he's in. He eats up the distance between us and drops to his knees beside the bed, right next to my pussy. Man has a front row seat to the show.

"What kind of help are you offering?" I tease as my soaked fingers are removed from my clenching core. They drip with my physical desire for them. Techy swiftly grabs my wrist and brings the digits to his mouth, sucking the coating clean off.

"You taste so fucking good," he groans around them. Again, there's a spasm that takes over my bottom half at his dirty words. Lust mixes in his gray eyes behind the surface. I can see him fighting himself between taking what he wants and asking for permission. He knows me well enough that asking for permission is entirely necessary.

"What kind of help?" I ask again, raising my eyes to meet Nomad's. His narrow on my bottom naked half, zeroing on the tattoo.

Suddenly, I no longer feel sexy or cute. I feel like the biggest idiot in the world. He catches himself, swallowing thickly and taking a single step away from me as I toss the blanket back over my naked half.

"I'm sorry," he says softly, not meeting my eyes. His hand rubs the back of his neck as Techy tries to figure out what just happened. "You don't have to talk about it, but..." he trails off.

"It's the brand," I whisper, the self-reflection suddenly turning ugly. "They said that I'd never be able to belong to anyone else since I was *theirs*. So, they branded me."

"You don't belong to anyone," Techy snarls fiercely next to me, sitting on his knees. "You are a grown woman with thoughts and feelings. You can do as you please." A watery giggle can't be helped at this man's loyalty.

He'd make a great feminist.

"It's not that easy," I say as my voice cracks. Clearing it several times, it doesn't move the lump sitting there.

"It's not easy, you're right," Nomad starts, sitting on the edge of my bed and taking my hand in his. Techy does the same on the other side, a determined look covering his features. "We'd never make you do something you're not comfortable with."

There's an overwhelming pause.

"I don't think I ever told you why I joined the MC, did I?" Techy asks softly, glancing over his shoulder at Nomad. Shaking my head, my eyes feel as wide as saucers. I sit up straighter, my heart hammering. Nomad reaches over and grabs his husbands hands, their black bands glinting in the low light.

Chapter Thirty-Three

EIGHT YEARS AGO

 TECHY

"*Shhh,*" *he hushes cheekily, my boyfriend kissing me harshly. His fingers dig into my scalp, the pleasurable pain radiating from his tugs. My boyfriend is a few years older than me at twenty two. He knew I just graduated high-school and still exploring my sexuality. Open and honest, he showed me the path to my true self. If it feels good, why stop?*

"You should leave before we get caught," I mutter as his teeth sink into my lower lip. With a blush like a schoolgirl, I peek my head out of the closet door. Checking that the coast is clear, we tip-toe to the main room where my father sits penrod straight.

His eyes gleam with burning rage. It's a look I am all too familiar with. Kent furrows his brows as my father stares straight ahead unmoving.

"Head home. I'll text you later," I mutter to Kent, pushing him gently toward the door. He flicks his gaze between myself and my father, confusion and worry etched in there. "I'll be fine, go," I plead, hoping he'll take the hint.

Thankfully, he does. The door closes quietly behind him. Neither of us move as we wait for Kent's car to start and fade into the distance.

Watching with rigid stiffness, I square my shoulders.

He knows.

"What were you doing in the closet, boy?" He quizzes, slowly standing and straightening his suit jacket. I debate between telling the truth and lying.

"He needed help finding a coat that was the right size. He'd forgotten his at home." Lie it is.

Before I can even register what's happening, he launches over the table.

"You lying slut," he snarls, his open palm slamming against my cheek. My knees threaten to give way as my head swings to the side from the force. Stumbling backward, the backs of my knees meet the ridge of the other table, causing me to fall backward. "No son of mine will ever be in sin!"

"What sins, father?" I shout, pretending to be utterly clueless. Instead of doing anything, he removes his phone from his pocket.

"Fuck, your ass is so tight." Kent's voice echoes around us as my voice sounds around us in rapture. He recorded us having sex... "Shit, you feel so damn good. Fuck, fuck," the recording keeps playing as my eyes slam shut in shame.

He stalks forward when the recording ends, crouching before me and wrapping his hands tightly around my throat.

"He is the devil who encompasses my son will be no longer!" He shouts, chanting it over and over again as my lungs stop getting air.

I claw against his hands with no purchase, Reaching up to his face, I dig my thumbs into his eyes. He rears back with a scream, giving me time to bolt. There's no time to grab anything as I race out of the door.

"God will never forgive you! Don't bring your unwashed sins back to this house!" He screams after me. Running at full speed, I don't look back to see if he's following me. That's a risk I won't take.

I don't stop until my lungs feel as though they're about to collapse from the exertion. Bending over, my world spins on its axis, struggling to get myself right again.

"Woah, you okay?" A deep voice draws. Bolting up right, I take a single step back, ready to start going again. A few large men stand there, arms crossed over their chests. We assess each other, trying to determine if either of us are threats.

"I..." I pause, looking around.

"There's no need to lie if you're not okay. Come on, let's go to the diner down the road." Father and I are extremely secluded in the mountains, so the fact that I made it this far means I'd been running for a while. A stirring in my gut is the only reason my legs start moving toward them. An air of safety oozes from them, a sense of security.

"My name is Rodger Sinclair. This is Nomad, one of the prospects we've taken under our wing, and Widower, my daughter." Widower is a short girl, but that doesn't mean I don't think she'd kick my ass. Nomad on the other hand...he looks like God's gift to women. Tall with short stubble curving his jaw. The man is a freaking statue.

Rodger must notice because he smirks. "Nomad can give you a ride, right kid?" He looks over at the man in question, his brow raised as a warning.

"Sure," he grunts, turning toward me again. His eyes are steel blue and hard. "You ever ridden before?"

"No," I mutter, embarrassment creeping in my bones. A flush goes from my neck to my ears, the heat radiating. He barks a quick laugh.

"Climb on behind me and hold on," he says, starting the bike and straddling the seat. I clamber onto it, keeping my hands on his shoulders. Almost like an act of frustration, he jumps the bike forward a bit. My body instinctively lurches to hang onto the burly man. Another core hardening laugh releases from him as I let go of a small smirk.

"You can take the stick out of your ass. You're safe with us," he says gently, looking over his shoulder. Before I can reply, Rodger takes off with Widower following in his wake. Nomad surges forward behind the string of bikes.

A sudden heady feeling of exhilaration takes over my senses, my eyes and cheeks are burning from the smile I'm sporting. Even my crotch is starting to stir in anticipation.

I think back to Kent, my boyfriend who wasn't out of the closet yet either. Both coming from distinguished families, it would put them to shame. I can't think about him right now. We both knew it wouldn't last. Plus, he said that we weren't really dating, that we were just friends with benefits. I was the hopeful one.

My perfectly styled hair is suddenly mussed up as he speeds up even more to catch up with the others. Letting out a shout of happiness, the sun clashes against my pale tone. It's a warm day out, one that needs to be cherished instead of isolated inside a stuff house.

He slows down, dipping into a small drive at the backroads diner. Letting me off, I work to not burn myself on the piping hot pipes. He chuckles as my odd hobble before kicking himself over the bike.

We lock eyes for a moment, something deep passing behind his gaze before a throat clears. Rodger stands there with a knowing smirk and *a thick gray brow raised. Another deep flush takes over my face as I try to dip my head and hide. A frilly giggle sounds, forcing me to snap up at the sound. Widower, the daughter, has her hands placed on her hips sassily.*

"You coming?" She asks, putting a double meaning behind her words. More laughter filters the small parking lot as Nomad throws an arm over my shoulders and leads us inside.

"What are you having?" He asks quietly, gazing down at the menu.

"Uhm, I didn't bring any money, so I'll just have water."

"Nonsense. Eat." Rodger orders. He doesn't look up at all.

"You heard the man, what'll it be?" Widower asks, leaning forward on her elbows. There's a mysterious twinkle in her eye as her gaze flitters between Nomad and I. It's almost...knowing?

"Uhm, just a burger is fine. Water." Another eye roll from the girl and she's ordering me a steak, medium well, with fries. Nomad doesn't let me argue at all.

"So, young man. What were you running from?" I sputter at Rodger's direct question. Water threatens to come up my nose, the burn like chlorine hitting my nostrils. "And again, don't think about lying."

More embarrassment and shame coat me. Thinking of ways to get out of this, Nomad seems to catch the drift.

"If I can guess it, you'll come back with us. If not, we'll take you wherever you want to go." With a thick swallow, I nod. His massive hand reaches over, clasping my smaller one in it.

"Deal," I croak, praying that he doesn't get it.

"You got kicked out for hiding something," he starts, assessing me fully. My shoulders stiffen on their own according, body jerking. "I'll

guess...you came out of the closet?" I shake my head, the lump making air struggle to hit my lungs.

"Not quite," I squeak. He takes a deep breath, looking around to the other two before leveling me once more.

"You were caught?" He whispers, his finger and thumb gripping my chin and tilting my head to look back at him. I nod. There's no point in denying it.

That same frilly laugh tinkles from across from us.

"Jesus, Nomad. If you weren't direct, I'd be concerned," she smiles, grabbing her own water. I follow suit with the hopes it'll clear the damn frog stuck in there.

"Well, good thing we're all about equality and love," Rodger snorts. I shoot to look up at him, but he doesn't return the gaze. He keeps it on his phone that he types away quickly on. "You got any skills?"

"Uhm, I'm pretty good with technology?" I say more as a question than a statement.

"How good?" He pauses, looking over at me with a raised brow.

"I hacked several big chain corporations for my father when he needed dirt planted," I mutter. I'm not exactly proud of things I've done in the past. Honestly, I've convinced myself that it's for survival.

"Nice," he praises, typing on his phone once more. A sound tinkers from it. With a wide smile, he flips the phone to show Widower, who looks just as happy.

"Welcome aboard," Nomad smiles tenderly. "You'll be with the tech crew."

Chapter Thirty-Four

Aspen

Tears stream down my face as he finishes his story. A choked sob leaks from me, and I decide this isn't the time to hold back. If anything, I need to prove to him, them, I'm willing for the next step.

In that case, I launch myself off the bed and into his body. Obviously not expecting it, he flails backward on the bed with me over top of him. In another plot twist, my lips land overtop of his. The immobility of my leg doesn't help anything, but it's oddly not that hard to work around when you're flexible.

"Shit, pretty girl," he huffs, his hands automatically landing on my hips to keep me still. It doesn't work once his lower region takes notice of where my crotch is.

"For someone who said I deserve everything," I pause, searching his eyes. "You deserve the world, and then some." His fingers gently fist in the back of my hair, bringing my mouth to meet his. It's a kiss that makes your knees go weak, stars burst behind your eyelids as they devour you. Instead of showing dominance, he pushes submission into it, showing me that he'd rather me be in charge.

The free hand slowly tangles around my waist. He keeps me locked to him without suffocating me.

A warm hand trails up my uninjured leg causally, swirling designs and patterns along the way. The sensation simply adds to the mixture of overwhelming pleasure. Ever since my first day in captivity, maybe even before, I'd never felt anything like this.

Both men suck the past right from the present. There's no worries about what happened before now or what is to come. Simply, we stay in the moment as my core clenches for more. Only the heat of this moment is on my mind, and I'll be honest, I have zero desire to think of anything else.

"One day," Nomad breathes, suddenly right next to my ear. "You're going to tell us about everything you went through." I suck in a ragged breath as I work to stay in the moment.

"In exchange," Techy mutters against my lips, sucking my bottom one between his teeth and biting. Hard. "We'll give you everything you ever wanted." Sitting back, I stare into the depths of gray swirls. I'd never noticed before, but there are flecks of gold accents. The other male, one that I'd never forget even if he let me, grabs my hand and brings my knuckles up for a kiss.

"You'll never be without again," he rasps. Love engulfs me as I realize...I'm falling in love with them. We may not have had that physical piece, but they've been proving to me time and time again that love isn't taught. It's earned. It's given. It develops and flourishes with the right amount of nourishment.

It's like maintaining an orchid. They saw me struggling, realizing that the soul was rotted and had no nutrients left. With the help of Doc, they de-rooted me from the moldy soil and slowly removed me. Then, they started to prune the negative foundation

I'd been growing on and give me a mixture of love and structure. They feed me, water me, and ensure I have enough brightness to my day.

"Thank you," I whisper, turning my hand over in Nomad's and clasping it tightly. "You have no idea how much this means to me." My stomach churns with need, the odd desire suddenly ramped up by these two men. If their love wasn't so fucking sexy...

"You know you're more," Nomad mumbles, his thumb caressing the back of my hand. "You're worthy of more."

"Please," I whimper. They both freeze, and I do too. It's like it slipped but intentionally forcing me to show my cards to them.

"Aspen," Techy groans with a pained expression. Leaning forward, I level his gaze with mine. A struggle battles behind his depths. While he wages war on himself, I turn and do the same to Nomad.

His deep blues are like steel, giving nothing away. I don't hold back. Everything I want to say, desperate to portray, is poured from my heart and through my eyes.

"Make it go away."

Something snaps inside both of them as Nomad dives toward us, careful not to hurt myself nor Techy. His hand cups my jaw, and brings me in for a searing, heart stopping kiss.

It's like air is not needed as he eats me up. There's no stopping, no slowing down. This is a run-away train, and I have no desire to be the one to pull the brakes. A second pair of familiar hands move my hair, plush lips taking over as wet kisses are placed on the pulse point in my neck. Their kisses are similar in the way they push what they feel through it, but this is different. He showers my heart with love, pushing past the dark clouds that threaten to overtake me.

Sunlight breaks through the barrier of darkness. He breathes life into me with his kiss, like zapping me with an electrical current.

Jerking back, I flicker between the two men. Their body language portrays complete mercy and submission, not quite something I'd see from historical encounters.

"What do you need from us?" Nomad asks, his fists clenching and jaw ticking. At first, I believe he's upset with me. Then, I watch his hands reach for me and stop, going back to his side.

My eyes flutter shut with a disgusted shiver. Several hands touch me in places that I don't want, forcing me to take their punishments and pleasures as my own. I can't help the chill that rakes over me.

"I just want it to go away. Make it stop," I plead. The two men glance between one another before Nomad stands from the bed.

"I'd like to teach you the safety of submission," Nomad suggests softly, holding out his calloused hand. "We won't be in the club, but I want you to know that you're in charge. What happens with us is controlled by you. The power is completely in your hands."

Bile rises in my throat at the thought. Being strung up, pushed toward a limit that I'm afraid of...

"Will you join us?" Techy asks from below me. I search his face, the honesty unwavering.

After several moments of silence, I decide that this may be my chance to let go. Be free from the chaos living inside of me, and choose things for myself for a change.

"Yes."

Chapter Thirty-Five

Aspen

Nomad lays me gently on his bed, his lips remaining locked with mine as he shows me the truth of what we're doing. There's nothing to be afraid of. Tipping my head to the side, he breathes wickedly into my neck, licking the pulse point. My eyes threaten to flutter shut until I catch sight of the window. Not the window itself, but the snow falling heavily to the ground.

"That's so beautiful," I whisper, a chill casting through me as both men blow cool air over the wet spot. Pure white snow coats the ground outside. A simplicity in the view makes my chest suddenly feel more free. Lighter than before. If I wanted, I could charge outside and dance in it. They'd only stop me to bundle me up. And ensure I'm not a trip hazard.

"Just like you," Techy whispers, kissing toward my temple. Nomad joins him, their mouths meeting in a searing kiss right above my ear. Nomad pulls away first, tugging his own lip as he focuses on me. Leaning down, he holds my gaze.

"Remember," he leans down and nibbles my ear, "you're in charge." Lightening zings through my core at the confession. With his wicked smirk, something inside my brain seems to snap. As if we were meant to be here all along.

"I want you to remember these words and what they mean," Techy starts, crawling onto the bed behind me. His shirt is nowhere to be seen, his glorious chest on display. He may not be made of muscle like Nomad, but he's nothing less than perfect. Biting the lobe of my other ear, goosebumps race across my skin at the pure need pooling in my panties.

I just want this to stop...

"Green," Nomad grunts, tugging the hem of my shirt upward. He waits for permission, which I grant without hesitation this time. "That means you're fine, you're good to keep going."

"Yellow," Techy follows quickly, fingering the latch of my bra. Another nod and it's popped off me, sliding down my arms to my elbows. Both men groan at the sight of my breasts. Scars litter the pale flesh. But I've decided that I'm going to brace for the point of no return. "Yellow means slow down or you don't like something, but not to stop completely."

Air whooshes from my lungs as Nomad bites into the soft flesh on my neck. There's no doubt of a mark appearing. Instead of mortification, it's almost...freeing. The pain seems to wash right into a soothing pleasure from them both caressing me. It's odd, because when I was in captivity, pain was pain. Pleasure simply didn't exist.

Now, there's pleasure in the pain itself.

"Red," they both say, stopping their ministrations completely. I lock eyes with Nomad as he drills his point home.

"Red means stop," he grunts, backing away slightly.

"We won't keep going or wait until the session is over. If you say red, we drop everything we're doing and go right into aftercare."

"Aftercare?" I ask, craning my neck to look over my shoulder at the man in question.

"Later." He stands up straight, his vest still hanging on for dear life. Muscles straining, the material falls down his shoulders and down his bulging arms. Saliva pools in my mouth as the odd desire to lick his veins burns the back of my mind. Sweeping over his figure, I suck my bottom lip between my teeth. I'd probably be cringing if I were more self-conscious. With these two, they'd probably congratulate me on something so ridiculous.

Before the vest falls to the floor, he brings it forward, folding it meticulously. The care he takes in ensuring it's not wrinkled sparks a weird maternal instinct. As if him folding clothes would make him the best fucking dad in the world.

Reaching behind himself, he fists the shirt in his hand and tugs. It easily comes up and over his head. It crumples to the floor in a heap, washing away my previous thoughts about how sexy folded laundry is. I can't tell if it's on purpose or not, but he glides his large hands down his pecs and over his abs, flexing beneath his fingers. Breath catching in my throat, I struggle to remain focused.

Just as I'm about to crawl toward him, another set of hands land smoothly on my hips. Much to my surprise, I don't even flinch. My body knows he's there, and that he's just not a threat. It's like light to dark, the difference his hands are to his husbands. While they're both rough and callous, Techy's are softer, smoother.

They dance at the hem of my sweats, playing with it but not making any moves to do anything about it. Opening my mouth, I'm just about to sass him when they start moving upward. They cup my small breasts, fitting perfectly with only a little bit of spillage on the sides.

"You're just a sight for sore eyes, pretty girl," Techy mutters in my ear, his breath tickling me in the best possible way. Shaking slightly, I lean my head back onto his shoulder. He turns his head and kisses my cheek, whispering words of encouragement as Nomad continues to strip before us.

"Your turn," Nomad demands, looking just past me to Techy. There's a wicked gleam in their eyes. Leaning me forward slightly, I'm shuffled around and put back to front with Nomad. My leg is still stuck in the brace, yet that doesn't seem to stop them at all.

Techy sits back on his knees, his bare chest heaving as he roams his own body erotically. If I didn't know any better, I'd think they're putting on a show for me. His own fingers dance in his hem the exact same time that Nomad's fingers do the same on mine.

"I bet if I dipped my fingers on your pussy, you'd be soaking wet," Nomad groans. An arm bands around my hips and yanks me backward into him more. I'm practically sitting on his lap with how close I am.

"I knew you were secretly a naughty girl," Techy teases, flicking the button undone and shimmying out of his pants. The boxers he sports do nothing to hide his raging hard on.

"I think she's going to make the naughty list this year, don't you?" Nomad asks, dipping a single finger under my pants and toying with the heated skin. "You don't want to be a good girl, do you?"

"No," I hum, one of my arms reaching up and back to grasp his neck. He chuckles mirthlessly into my neck, kissing the spot he'd ruthlessly sucked on.

"Well, you're in for a treat. You've made the top of *Satan's Naughty List*, baby girl." His tattooed hand wraps loosely around the front of my throat. Again, I expect my body to immediately reject the idea. Instead, it relishes in the touch. Core clenching with desire, Nomad pushes his hand inside my pants. Strong fingers toy with me through the lacy material. He fucking purrs behind me. One that rumbles our bodies and sends vibrations straight to my clit.

"Color?" Techy asks, crawling toward us one again. Confusion envelopes me for a moment before I realize he's referring to my safe words.

"Green," I gasp, the intoxicating feeling of Nomad's fingers strumming my most sensitive place taking me closer to an edge that I've been deprived of for so long.

"I would say you're a good girl, but the noises you're making say otherwise." I don't even realize I'm quivering until this very moment, the knot of desire getting tighter and tighter.

"Are you going to give me your first orgasm, pretty girl?" He drawls, slowing his fingers. A deep breath fills my lungs, patience suddenly a virtue.

"Yes," I croak. He pauses all together, pulling his fingers out completely.

"Yes, what?" An air of dominance comes crashing off him, the sense of submission immediately seeping into my bones. Being naughty means punishments, but I don't think I want those from him. I want to be his naughty girl in all the good ways.

"Yes, sir."

Chapter Thirty-Six

NOMAD

C hest filling with pride, I force myself not to let the intoxicating power overcome my senses. As a team, Techy and
I work to shimmy her pants off and over her brace. Flashes cross
her eyes, leaving as quickly as they came. It concerns me, and I
ensure that I'm wholeheartedly keeping track of her emotions and
feelings. She wants us to help her get through this, help her make
the demons go away. Even if only for a little while.

Neither of us can afford to be off our A-game.

"Good girl," I rasp, cupping her perfect tits in my hands. It's like
they were made exactly for my hands. They're heavy with pert pink
nipples that make my mouth water. My wonderful husband crawls
expertly between her parted legs. One arm skillfully takes her good
leg and flings it over his shoulder, her braced leg spread out a bit
to ensure it doesn't get hurt. Bringing one hand to her throat, I
wrap it gently around, caging her body against mine. She tenses for
a moment before relinquishing the hold on herself. Techy keeps a
close eye on her with the move, flicking his eyes with praise as she
takes it.

As far as I know, he's never even tasted pussy. When we have our go-arounds, it's either another man or I'm the one indulging the woman. Either way, I'm mixed with shock and lust as his tongue does one, long slow lick through her slit.

"Usually we'd have a conversation about this..." Techy rumbles in satisfaction. His tongue darts out, lapping happily at her clit. She writhes in my arms, gyrating her hips against his face as he pushes her closer and closer to her freedom. Pleasurable noises fall from her, head falling back on my shoulder.

Just as she's about to crest over the hill, Techy pulls back. "That is one delicious pussy." Using his fingers, he scoops up some of her cum and brings it to my lips. She catches the glint in the pale moonlight as Techy pushes the coated digits into my mouth. I lap at them like a starved man.

A feral growl and my hand tightening slightly, she purrs her own satisfactory sound.

"If I'd known you tasted so good, I'd have you for all three courses, plus snacks," I rumble, bringing my head down to kiss her. It's an awkward angle, but it gets the job done. Her lips are ripped away from mine as my husband devours the beauty between us. Her juices coat her face from the transfer, his own hand gripping her breast tightly as he tweaks her nipples.

"Color?" I ask, pressing wet kisses along her neck.

"Green, green," she chants, trying to move her hands to our bodies. I snatch one while my husband snatches the other. Bringing them together, I reach over and grab a red silk ribbon. Her eyes snap open at the grazing material. She doesn't say a word, her eyes a mixture before horror and appreciation.

"Does our naughty girl want to be tied up?" Techy asks, grabbing her jaw and tipping her head further back. She tries to nod, but the angle isn't letting her. "Words."

"Yes, sir," she strains.

"Naughty girl," he praises, quickly working the ribbon around them. "Next time you don't answer us, you'll be smacked right here." His hand drags over the tops of her breasts before a shallow swap hits the underside.

She jumps, uncertainty coating her hazel eyes. Yet, she doesn't ask us to stop nor slow down. With a startled jump, Techy leans down and snatches a pink, perky nipple between his lips.

"Ooooh," she sighs, her heavy melting into me as he bites and sucks her nipple until it's solid.

"More, please," she begs, her iris blown out with need.

"Good girl for asking," I praise, trailing a hand down her taut body to the junction between her thighs. Flicking over her swollen bud, I work it faster and faster. Undulating her hips, she doesn't waste any time in grabbing my wrist and keeping it where she wants it.

"Cum for us, pretty girl," Techy demands, circling a single finger at her entrance. Just as he goes to push inside, she explodes. It's like he pulled the pin and the grenade detonated.

"Yes!" She shrieks, eyes rolling to the back of her head as her legs shake in ecstasy. It takes her several moments to come back down from her high, eyes blinking slowly.

"You're so sexy when you cum." Nibbling her ear, my rock hard cock pushes into her back even more.

"They stopped..." she whispers, looking over her shoulder at me. "Make them go away. Completely."

"I can't promise anything, sweetheart," I mutter, cupping her face and bringing my lips to hers. Techy seems to think that's the perfect time to start licking her pussy again. A jump and moan later, she's writhing away.

"I want your cocks," she demands, narrowing her gaze on us both. "Please make it stop." Techy and I share a look before he nods. Reaching over to the nightstand, he stops for a brief moment.

"We don't have any condoms, sweetheart. We usually don't have to worry about..."

"I know. It's fine, I'm clean. Doc checked. Please," she begs, trying to push herself into him. Another look and he's giving into her.

"Lean back against Nomad." She does as asked, her back against my front again. Grabbing her injured leg gently, I tilt backward and carefully lay us flat. It's in the air while her other ankle is grabbed by Techy. He passes it to me, silently asking me to hold her open for him. Rubbing himself against her opening, she wriggles against me as she attempts to scoot further down my body.

"You still need to be careful," I hint with a tone of authority. Immediately she stops moving. "He will give it when he's ready, won't you?"

"Yes, sir," he agrees, catching her gaze with his. Taking the head of his cock, he flicks it over her clit. Loving the feeling, her body tenses again.

"Ready?" He mutters, and I watch her eyes roll back as his body comes closer and closer. Finally, his heavy sac hits the underside of my own hard member. "This okay?" His voice is strained as he keeps himself from moving. She doesn't say anything for long moments. We share a look before he pulls out completely and sits on his heels.

"Don't stop," she sobs, eyes still tightly shut.

"Open your eyes," I bark. She flings them open, looking almost dazed. "When asked a question, you will answer. Are you okay?"

"Yes!" She screams, taking her tied hands and throwing them backward. "Make them go away!" She shrieks, aggression suddenly laced into her movements.

Techy wastes no time, impaling the sweet girl in our arms. Instead of slow movements, he rears back and slams into her over and over again. A wickedness haunts his eyes as he dominates the girl between us.

"More!" She shouts. Her hips wiggle as I reach between us and pinch her clit. I figured that would be what sends her over the edge, but it's not. Chanting over and over again that she needs more, Techy stops.

"What do you need more of?"

"I want you both! Please," her eyes are wide as she begs.

"Are you sure?" I ask, whispering in her ear. Like a slap, she whips her head to the side.

"If I wasn't okay, I'd tell you," she growls out, like a little demon possessed. It's fucking hot.

"Your wish is our command, naughty girl." Techy takes the initiative to lube me up, notching me at her entrance. He assists her in sitting up and putting her hands on my chest. Practically folded in half, I tilt my hips upward and sink fully inside of her.

She's tighter than a vice grip trying to milk me.

After a few pumps I pause, letting my husband push a finger inside with me.

"Oh fuck," she hisses, head tipping backward. The sound would concern me if it wasn't made from pure bliss.

"You're so tight, pretty girl," he coos, shoving a second finger inside of her.

"Please fuck me," she begs, her lips pursed in pleasure. He leans forward, taking his lips in his as his fingers curl around her sweet spot.

"There it is," he teases, rolling them around inside of her. Just as she's about to rocket through her orgasm, he stops.

"Quit fucking doing that," she snaps.

"You're definitely going on the naughty list." He doesn't give her a chance to retort as he pushes inside. "Fuck," he drawls, eyes rolling as her pussy gets tighter and tighter. Like the vixen she is, she squeezes around us both as her own wanton noises echo off the walls.

His own flex upward, which seems to hit *the spot*.

"Yes!" She screams. With no warning, our cocks are practically pushed out of her pussy as she squirts all over Techy's abdomen.

Holy shit.

Leaning down, he pushes two fingers inside of her channel and harshly works them. More liquid comes pouring out of her as she screams through her climax. Removing his sopping digits, he flicks them over her body before shoving himself and I back into her.

We don't give her a chance to catch her breath as we pound forcefully inside of her. Techy grabs her good leg, letting me drop my hand and send a few searing smacks to the sensitive bud.

My own balls dry tightly into my body as the familiar sensations start to tingle.

"Cum for us, naughty girl," I growl into her ear, taking two fingers and rubbing her nub harshly. Another vocal climax rips out of her as she grips us tightly.

"Oh shit," I grunt, pushing into her a couple more times with Techy. Hips stuttering, I roar my release. My sexy husband follows suit, pouring ourselves inside of her like heathens.

An odd sensation lands inside my chest, almost a primal one at the very possible chance that this could get her pregnant.

If she didn't have her shit removed, idiot.

Shaking the thought and feelings away, I put several gentle kisses to her sweat soaked hair. Techy and I both shower her with praises before he gets off to retrieve a warm cloth. It doesn't take her mere seconds before she completely passes out against me.

Chapter Thirty-Seven

 TECHY

Nomad and I both fully expected her to run. Hide in a corner somewhere and rock on her butt like they do in horror movies. Much to our surprise, and the amount of pride for her improvement, she sleeps soundly between us. The comfort level she has is evident since she zonked seconds after we finished, then didn't even stutter as we moved her around.

He brushes her hair away from her face. Soft snores ooze out of her relaxed state. No pinched brows, confused expressions, or the odd fearful glance. She's just...serene.

"She feels the same," he mutters, leaning down to place a gentle kiss on her forehead. Usually, he's hard as stone, his exterior stoic in an effort to fend off assholes around us. With her? He's merciful, meeting her scared looks with reassurance of his own. My heart warms with the idea that she could easily fit with us. Even with the interactions we've had, she's literally perfect.

"I think I'm falling in love with her," I confess, looking down at the sleeping angel in our arms. She stirs a little, a small sigh falling from her lips. The sound is one of contentment.

The feeling is mutual, pretty girl.

"I am too," Nomad mumbles. Tipping his head up, he leans over her small body and catches my lips against his. It's not a horny kiss, not one fueled by passion.

"I love you," the small girl whispers, causing the two of us to jerk backward. Tears pool in her sweet hazel eyes, her blinks slow. I almost wonder if I'm simply imagining it. Maybe she's still asleep...both her hands reach up and grasp our cheeks.

"Pretty girl," Techy sighs, shaking his head. Her hands roam further back, tangling in our hair.

"I love you both," she announces. "You both..." she stops, her throat thick with emotion.

"You don't have-"

"Yes, I want to," she interrupts Nomad. "Please let me." We all swallow heavily, almost in unison.

He nods, glancing up at me. I give him an affirmative nod. We help her sit up higher, careful not to jostle her leg around. The pillows are adjusted under her once again.

"You two have been...substantial in helping me get better." Nomad wants to say something, but he thankfully stays quiet. "If it weren't for you when I was kidnapped...I don't know if I would have survived. With nothing to look forward to, the darkness nearly consumed me in its entirety."

"That's very poetic, sweetheart." Nomad's grin is full of teeth, and it fully meets his eyes as he surges love toward the woman beneath us.

"Oh hush," she retorts, swatting him playfully. Catching the hand, he smoothly brings it to his mouth and kisses her knuckles. A deep red blush creeps along her skin, so bright that the pale moon finds it in the dark.

"Before you both, the dark consumed me. My heart was so cold, iced out and black as coal. There was no room for love or affection as it was at full capacity simply trying to carry on. Living another day was like reliving your worst nightmares, constantly being surrounded by those who wish you unwell. My life was as uneven as a continuous earthquake. I was forced to stumble around, until finally...you found me. There was an opening, and I knew if I didn't run, I'd die. So, I took it. And you found me."

Tears prick my eyes at her words. While they're dramatized, she's not exactly wrong. I've not experienced the level of trauma she has, but we've both seen darkness. All of us have.

Glancing at Nomad, he reflects how we all feel too.

"You're one of the strongest women I know," he mutters, leaning down to kiss her softly.

"I think I'm ready to talk about it..." she whispers, flicking between us. While we know bits and pieces, we've not gotten the whole story.

"Again, you don't have to..." she grasps the back of my head and pulls me to join their kiss.

"I want to."

Chapter Thirty-Eight

Aspen

AGE SIXTEEN

Giggling, Cynthia opens the top to her convertible, letting our hair fly in the breeze. Mom and dad didn't have money to get my own car, but that's alright. My best friend, Cynthia, prefers to drive us everywhere anyway.

"Whoooo!" I scream, arms flailing above my head as we cruise through downtown. Old people look our way, we're practically unstoppable.

"Girl, can you believe we're going to be seniors in a few months?" She shrieks, happily driving us toward my place. Dad asked for me to be home by seven today, which is super early, but since I'm rarely home, it's fine.

"I literally can't!" I laugh, my cheeks hurt from the amount of smiling. Graduation is tonight, and we'll be free for the rest of the summer before we start back up again. She got a summer job in Texas

working for her family. It's more like an internship, but it'll look great on her resume! I tried to get my parents to let me go. They said they wanted me closer to home. Sad as it is, and the missed opportunity for amazing career building, I can get a job around here. I haven't looked yet, but I'll start searching next week.

She swings the car around the corner, music blasting through the radio as the wind muses up our hair. Clasping hands, we slow outside my house. There's a black SUV sitting outside, which isn't uncommon. Dad has associates around a lot to talk business. It's boring, and I'm usually dismissed to my room.

Leaning over, I give her a squeezing hug. I won't see her all fucking summer! Life is so unfair sometimes.

"*Stay safe this summer, yeah?*" *I mumble, tightening just a smidge. She returns the embrace, tears leaking down her cheeks.*

"*Fuck off! You know I will, little Miss Virgin,*" *she teases. She shoves my shoulder and dabs her eyes. "Now get out of my car before I start crying my ass off." Laughing, I grab my bag and clamber out.*

"*Love you girl.*" *With a quick blow-kiss, I head up the drive. There's someone sitting in the driver's seat as I walk by, his eyes narrowed and sour. I scowl back at him, flipping my hair over my shoulder.*

Creepy fucking men.

Tiptoeing into the main living space, there's a shuffle and a sharp smack that causes a muffled cry. I peek my head around the corner only to find my mom and dad tied back to back in their chairs. I can't see my mother, I can only see her bleached blonde hair from behind. My father on the other hand, has something shoved in his mouth and strapped in place with a rope. It's like a make-shift gag.

Keeping my tone down, I do my best to stay silent. Hopefully the weird dude in the car doesn't tell them I came in.

I back around the corner and turn on my heel, only to run right into a man built like a fucking wall. He's wearing black on black, his suit pristinely pressed to perfection. Snapping his hand out, he grips my upper arm tightly. Too tightly.

"Let go, fucker," I hiss, trying to pull out of his grip. Unfortunately, it's like a fucking vice around my arm.

"Shut up," he grunts, his other hand swinging out and effectively silencing me with a slap. Something on my face, I'm not entirely sure what, makes a popping noise. Liquid trickles down my chin. It doesn't take a fucking doctor to know it's blood.

His fist clenches even tighter, no doubt leaving a bruise in its wake, hauling me to the drawing room where my parents are strapped together.

"What's going on?" I shriek, tugging against his grip. I don't need the details to know this isn't a good situation. Not at all. "Get your hands off of me you fucking twatwaffle!"

"Shut her up." I snap up to see one of my father's main associates sitting in the dingy chair. He looks at his polished fucking nails like he's the king of the world against us scum.

Opening my mouth to tell him off, the handsy guy shoves his handkerchief into my mouth. I gag lightly at the tough cotton, trying to force it back out. It doesn't give as a piece of tape slaps over my lips.

How fucking cliché.

"It's a family reunion," Rodney cheers with a loud clap. Brushing imaginary dirt off his suit, he stands and reaches for handsy. They exchange a folder, pushing it in front of me first. "You know who

this is, don't you?" Staring at the photo, I flicker around in utter confusion.

It's a photo of me staring back. I'm with a group of my friends shopping. From what it looks like, I'm grinning right into the camera lens. The shot is candid, so I wasn't posing for it.

I nod, distrust immediately churning in my gut. He grabs the folder back before flipping to another page. It's me and my friends shopping. I'm sliding the black card out of the reader with a grin. Again and again, he shows me pictures of me shopping.

"You see a trend, right?" I ask, stopping on the last photo. It's a document of our card statements. We're not rich, but I worked my ass off for my money. Put it into my bank by myself. I didn't have access to the account because I'm not old enough, or at least that's what they told me. I thought I was spending my own money. Turns out, according to the papers in front of me, they were spending my money to 0.

I can't look at them from how I'm sitting, but I can feel their eyes on the back of my body.

"Daddy and Mommy appear to have a bit of a problem," he muses, snapping the file closed. I can't take my eyes off the spot on the table. "I bet you're wondering what this means?" I nod, tears welling in my eyes as assumptions start rolling through me.

Unfortunately, what he says next is something I would have never guessed.

"Their debts are paid if you marry me." Startled, my brows furrow deeply on my forehead. What the fuck would he want with a sixteen year old girl?

I crane to look at my parents, resentment and anger fusing deep within me. They'd give me up...for money?

The tape is suddenly ripped off my mouth, skin being taken with it. "I don't understand," I sob, tears streaming down my cheeks.

"You'll be married to me, darling. Don't you worry. You'll be well taken care of."

AGE NINETEEN

"Time of death?" The man asks, looking down at his nose at me. I have tears streaming down my face. What he doesn't know is that it's from fear.

"I-I-I don't know," I sob, knees crumbling as the weight lifts from my shoulders. Rodney lies so still on his bed, unmoving. Unbreathing. A riot of freedom seems to kickstart in my brain. The man hums, grabbing Rodney's wrist once more to check for a pulse. Again, nothing.

"Servant," one of the enforcers barks. My spine jerks pin-rod straight. Clambering to my feet, I put the emotional facade back on. Overwhelming hatred. Fear. Freedom. I can feel it all suddenly wanting to break the dam I so carefully constructed.

"You'll be reassigned, dear," a short woman says from the top of her nose. She looks down on me with a mixture of sweetness and as if I'm the scum on the bottom of her shoes.

"Yes, madam," I nod with a sharp curtsy. The heavy weight from Rodney's ring feels like a rock, one that would force me to drown if dropped in water. I can handle being reassigned as a maid...that's not terrible. It's better than this.

Rodney said my will was too strong for him, but would be great for his heir...luckily and unfortunately all at the same time, an heir wasn't blessed to us. Two short nights ago, Rodney tried to...

I can't even say it, my body still wracking with fearful shivers. My life flashed before my eyes. So, I decided to take matters into my own hands. No one would ever know...

"Pack your bags, girl," the woman barks out, turning on her heel and walking back to the foyer. I try not to show my excitement.

Racing up the steps, I pack my things in a trunk offered by the enforcer. He stands nearby, obviously my watcher. It takes everything not to shout from the roof-tops that this actually fucking worked!

Clasping the clutch shut, he grunts a syllable or two and grabs it from where it's perched on the bed. It almost didn't close with how full it is.

"May I ask where we're going?" I mutter timidly. This man still scares the ever living shit out of me. He's not done anything since I was off limits, but now that the boss is dead....

"No." That's the end of that. Tossing the trunk into the boot of the car, he steps inside the driver side and turns it on. I don't wait for him to open it.

Off to my new life.

"Here's the new whore," the enforcer spits, shoving me forward. I stumble, only to be caught by a handsome man. His face is full with a beard, his teeth slightly starting to yellow, but that could be from the liquor these posh men tend to guzzle.

"Oh, I'm sure she's not that bad," he tsks. Taking a step backward, he peruses down my body.

"Beg to differ, she killed the boss." My head snaps toward him in shock that I quickly morphe into outrage.

"Watch what you accuse a lady of!" I retort, clasping my fingers in front of me like I was taught during those damn lessons. He snorts, shaking his head.

"Good luck with her. I hear she's feisty in bed." He snaps his teeth at me, biting his bottom lip before turning on his heel. We all watch in baited silence as he takes his leave.

"Gosh," I sigh, placing a hand on my head. Fake til' you make it. "I'm parched. Do you gentlemen have anything a lady can drink?" The two men perched behind beard guy give one another a look. It's one that's oddly familiar, my instinct telling me to run. Just as I'm about to take off, the tanned guy lurches for me. His hand tangles in my hair, and I halt with a shriek.

"Get off me!" It's no use. Several hands are on my shoulders, forcing me to kneel. There's a dark look in all of their eyes. My stomach sinks as everything catches up to me.

This is no better than before.

AGE TWENTY-FOUR

Counting the tiles on the ceiling, a spark smack hits my back somewhere. It jolts me from my daze, making me groan for having to re-count the damn things. Usually I get one-hundred and eight tiles, but today I only got one-hundred and three.

"*That's right whore, make some fucking noise.*" I can't really tell who's voice that is. My ears are plugged with water, or whatever they used to suffocate me. Foggy and winded, I don't have the energy any-more. Hanging my head low, their hands grope and grab, tugging on me and trying to get something I initially fought. Something I did not offer willingly.

Shutting my eyes, I let myself come out of my body. It's like watch-ing a movie of myself being tormented. My face is bruised, black and blue. Wrists bound behind my body, tilted upward as far as my shoulders will allow and feet tied apart with a bar. I purposefully turn around and refuse to see what's happening to myself.

"*I think she needs a reminder of who she belongs to.*" One set of hands leaves me, the door slamming behind whoever that was. I catch a glimpse of his beard from where I stand outside of myself. Charles left. Ravi and Stephan continue their myriad of things that I refuse to acknowledge. Blood trickles from between my thighs from their relentless torment. Again, refuse to even think about it.

A sharp buzzing snaps me from my dreaming, forcing me to focus. No matter how hard I try, I can't detach. Can't disassociate again.

I can't process what's happening before a searing pain radiates on my skin. A small area on my thigh burns like my flesh is being ripped apart ever-so-slowly. Screaming in outrage and pleading for mercy, he seems to only dig the needle further in.

"*Heavy handed asshole,*" I growl, wiggling around to get him to back off. This just pisses him off more.

"*Keep her occupied,*" he orders the other two. They tear and grab at my clothes, ripping them off completely. That's all it takes for me to step back outside of myself.

Chapter Thirty-Nine

NOMAD

My heart hurts for the girl below me. She didn't have to go into explicit details for us to know what happened. Techy and I both dive toward her, cradling her sobbing body against us. I'm sure that wasn't even a quarter of what she'd gone through, but here we are. Surviving. Thriving. *Living.*

"You're so strong, pretty girl," Techy praises, nuzzling his nose with hers. "Who knew we needed you as much as you needed us."

"He's right, sweetheart," I whisper. My lips nibble her ear, sucking the lobe gently. "You're more than we ever thought we needed." My nose rubs against hers. Techy grabs my jaw gently, pulling me over her body for another kiss before he gazes back down at her.

Sorrow and tenderness seep from his gray orbs into her deep hazel ones, his adoration clear as day. If we're being honest, I'm sure my eyes paint a similar picture.

"I love you." His eyes remain trained on hers, the hazel ones are wide and staring into his gray ones. Between them passes so many different emotions, it's hard to even keep up.

"I love you," I repeat, placing a gentle kiss against her cheek. Glancing up over my husband's shoulder, the snow circles the window seal, a large circle of frost taken over on the ridges. It's silent, no howling wind or roaring snow threatening to cause power outages. No, just a slow fall of flakes that cast upon one another, piling higher and higher.

A small hand grabs my chin, pulling me to look at her. No hesitation needed. Slanting my lips over hers, I do what Techy's eyes did to her. Careful not to crush her, I bear my weight down. A heady moan passes between us, the soft declaration enough to know she's not hurting. Her soft lips part as my tongue slips between them. Hands trail over our entwined bodies as she pushes upward into me. Naked breasts, heavy and full, tease my naked chest as her nipples turn to diamonds.

Suddenly, her mouth clashes harder against mine, as if she's waging a war between our lips. At first, I think nothing of it, until a whimper of satisfaction has her pulling away from me altogether. One hand flies downward, latching onto Techy's hair. Her nipple is gone, disappearing between his lips as his jaw rolls and flexes.

"Yes, Techy," she sighs, her hips rolling.

Popping off, he gazes up at her. "Paxton," he mutters, kissing up her body and planting a heart stopping kiss. "Call me Pax."

"Please, Pax." Like any good male, he can't deny what she's asking. It's like watching a porno right in front of me, except they're making love. This isn't just a kiss or an encounter like others before her.

This is real.

"Can I?" I rasp, walking my fingers down her tiny body. She's gained a little bit of weight since she's gotten here and since she's been back, but it's so much better than she was before.

"Please..." she trails, waiting patiently. My brain immediately starts misfiring. Pax told her his name, not just the name we dubbed him for the club. Names hold power and title. Someone could break you simply from knowing your *name*.

But I love her. There's no doubt about how much this female means to me. And if I had to trek through hail and high water, I'd do it in a heartbeat.

Swallowing thickly, I try to tell her a few times, but nothing comes out. It's a label I haven't touched since I joined the club. The only time it was used was when Pax and I got married. Other than that, I'm just Nomad. Lost and wandering in search of my home.

Except, I found my home in Pax, and now I've extended that home to Aspen.

"Drew." The words tumble out with a shiver down my spine. "Andrew." She doesn't even flinch while I stumble over myself.

"Thank you, Paxton and Andrew." Her head falls back onto the pillow, petting our cheeks lovingly. That odd swelling in my chest seems to take over again. It's a feeling I'd only felt with these two, but it seems to be growing hotter as I take in the beauty.

She *knows* us.

She accepts us.

She is one of us.

She ran for her life, only to run straight into our arms.

If it were up for me to decide, I'd say meeting her was a holiday miracle.

Chapter Forty

FIVE YEARS LATER

"Jesus Christ," I shout, halting as a paintball wallops me in the chest. "You little shits!" Running after my niece and nephews, they giggle and shriek in mock fear. Sebastian is only five, so I'm pretty careful with him. Axel, on the other hand, is freaking ten years old. That kid has better aim than my lazy eye. Ophelia is a little more sensitive, but she's a little bad ass.

Another ball slams into the backing of my chest piece causing me to stumble forward and land funny on my bad knee. With a hiss, I try to move out of the way before I can get stamped on.

"You alright?" A deep drawl asks from above me. My husband Nomad, the burly man that he is, has his beard braided into two parts thanks to me. He didn't care as long as I didn't dye them pink.

"I landed funky on my knee," I pout, trying to straighten out. It doesn't hurt too badly, but knowing my husbands, I can get them to do my bidding. Bending down, he scoops me up bridal style as Techy continues to target the kids. Once he sees me in Nomad's arms, he stops and rushes over, effectively leaving himself wide open for the kids.

"Fuckers," he grumbles as he scans my body over. "What happened?"

"She was being lazy, decided to fake a knee injury." Whipping my head around, my jaw drops in mock horror. "Don't even pretend, sweetheart. You love those boys, but I can tell you're getting anxious to leave."

"It's just too loud," I mutter, a wave of shame crashing over me. Hudson brought the boys so Nomad and Techy could have time with them. We've been out since nine this morning, and it's getting close to dinner time.

"Don't feel bad, pretty girl," Techy smiles, pushing a stray strand of hair behind my ear. Leaning in, his lips nibble on my lobe. "I would be lying if I said you being covered in paint wasn't the sexiest thing I've seen."

"Kids!" Hudson booms, laughing his ass off. Again, redness sparks over my skin.

"We'll be by next week for dinner?" Techy asks while assisting me in getting the damn vests off.

"Sounds good. Widower is on bedrest right now."

"You guys need to keep it in your pants," Nomad snorts. "This is baby six?" Using my fingers, I name off all the kids to only land on five. This would be six.

"She threatened me, said I was getting snipped," he laughs, shaking his head. "I told her those things aren't foolproof. She doesn't care."

"Well, here's to praying for stopping at six." They all hug while I remain in shock. I can't believe she'd willingly pop six kids out of her coochie.

About three years ago, the guys and I decided to take the plunge. We went to a fertility specialist who confirmed that I'd been given a hysterectomy. They reassured me that my ovaries were still in place, so my hormones should be okay. I cried my eyes out for days, then on and off for a few months. I mourned the choices that were ripped away from me.

Now, I'm kind of glad I didn't have the option. Hearing of how sleepless nights are, the constant feeding and changing, then the older kids talking back...I'd have backhanded my kid if he talked to me the way Axel talks to his mom. She puts him in his place, but she does it without abusing her damn kid.

I used to get my mouth washed out with soap. Apparently, that's frowned upon now.

Either way, we decided to live vicariously through others, mainly Hudson and Widower. Maggie and Crusher didn't have any other kids besides their twins, but I'm not really close with those two.

"What are you thinking about, sweetheart?" Nomad purrs, bringing hip lips to my ear.

"About how lucky I am to have you in my life," I retort. My lips brush against his, but I pull back before he can fully plant them.

"Damn right you are, we're fucking great," Techy says, fist pumping the air. They put their stuff away and walk me to the car. Nomad refuses to put me down, saying I'm a tripping hazard and should be looked after closely.

Not that I'm complaining.

Just as Techy opens the car door, I lean into Nomad's ear a bit more. Taking the lobe, I breathe gently.

"I'm also thinking about how my two husbands are going to teach me a lesson on being good."

I'm fucking thrown onto the bed, my two males undressing faster than I can catch my breath. Their eyes are hungry, blazing with need. There's not much I can do at this point besides stare. I want to strip, but I don't want to get into too much trouble.

We're still working on appropriate punishments for when I'm bad. There are kinks that need to be ironed out, but overall, they're gentle and understanding while still putting the brat inside of me back in her box.

"Why are you not stripping?" Techy asks, crawling next to me on the bed. Tracing a single finger on the sheets, I shrug.

"No one gave me any orders," I smile innocently. I may be full of shit, but I'm not wrong.

"Fine," Nomad drawls, taking a predatory step forward. "I want you naked in less than ten seconds, or I'll have you bent over my knee with ten spankings." Music to my fucking ears. Debating on whether to purposefully make the time run out, I decide against it. Brat me wants to make them work, but horny me says fuck them *now*.

Clothes go flying as I get naked for their eyes. I've gained significant weight, in which the guys tell me over and over again that they simply adore my new curves. I even slapped Nomad upside the head once because he said it gave *more cushion for the pushing.*

My back meets the silky material beneath me as Nomad's hulking figure crawls over top of me. His cock springs to life, bobbing and ready to make his entrance. Techy comes up beside me and grabs my arm to steady me as he moves me over top of him. No warning given, he pushes his thick cock inside of me. A burn stretch that switches into a drawn out moan from the both of us.

Once to the hilt, he uses his hips to move and pump me closer to the edge.

"Look at how she sucks you in," Nomad murmurs, his hands running over my inner thighs. His fingers trace my newest tattoo on the outer part of my thigh, covering the marking where *they* tried to claim me.

It's a stack of books with some flowers on it. It signifies the freedom I have and the ability to flourish, just like I can be free when I read or when a flower blooms.

While my mind wanders, Nomad takes the opportunity to rim my asshole. We don't do a ton of anal play, saying that Techy is great for that, but on the occasion that I need the release...they're definitely willing.

Making entrance inside my ass, his knuckles pop around the tight rim.

"Yes, Drew," I coo, my head tipping backward and landing on Techy's shoulder. Using his other hand, Nomad starts to slowly play with my clit.

"That's right, let me in," he groans, adding another finger to the mix. "Such a naughty girl." His hand rears back and slaps my pussy lightly. Techy makes a throaty sound as my walls squeeze him tightly.

"Put me in her ass," he grits out, teeth clashing together. Nomad doesn't hesitate to move Techy's big cock and notches it at my entrance. "Let me in, pretty girl. Let me own that ass."

It's fucking over for me.

Reprieve doesn't come as he notches inside the muscles before shoving himself harshly. Tears sting my eyes, my mind screaming with pain as he slowly moves. It quickly morphes into something more pleasurable, but fucking my ass is never an experience without a bit of pain in it.

"Get in here, baby," Techy calls, keeping himself tightly hilted to my bottom. Our husband scoots further up the bed and flicks his length over my clit. It takes everything inside of me not to let the ball of tension snap in my lower stomach.

Finally, he too makes his way inside of me. Stars burst behind my eyes as I explode. He didn't do anything except push in.

"Yes," I chant until I sag backward.

"I think you can do more," Techy mutters as his large hands grab the backs of my thighs and spread me wide. "Get up on your hands."

Nomad helps get me situated before he rocks backward while Techy rocks inward. The fullness never stops between them as one of them is always filling me.

At this point, I don't know where my toes start and my head ends. Or is that the other way around?

"Fuck, you're so damn tight." The tension peaks once again, faster than I wanted.

"Shit!" I scream, liquid pouring from my lower half as I cover Nomad with my juices. This seems to be the tipping point for them as they both roar out their own releases.

"I fucking love you, pretty girl," Techy sighs, placing gentle kisses on my neck while I lay like a limp noodle.

"I love you, sweetheart," Nomad follows as his lips land on mine. "Ever since that day, you really have been our walking miracle. Who knew that one shitty season would bring so many good ones?"

About the Author

Lexi Gray is an Alaskan-Based author with several years of free-lance editing under her belt. Ms. Gray has also dabbled in nar-rating, which can be found on Audible. She's had a passion for writing at an early age; however, started out in helping authors develop their writing skills and bringing languid movement and passion to their works. Her unique voice shines through her works, using emotion-based writing and hitting subjects that may present as taboo. Ms. Gray utilizes critical thinking and good, dirty and dark humor to get through it all.

Her hope is that when readers pick up her works, or the works of others she's helped along the way, they'll be stuck with their nose in it.

Ms. Gray herself enjoys reading dark romance, but also loves to dive into a dirty RomCom or two. From her own past experiences, she hopes to use her books as a sense of learning for those who read it, even if they end up only holding it with one hand along the way...IYKYK.

You can check out updates along the way on her Instagram: @AuthorLexiGray or on her website at AuthorLexiGray.com

Acknowledgements

Of course, first and foremost, I want to thank the amazing readers who take the time to pick this up! You all continue to make my dreams come true, and I can't be more honored with hearing the amazing things you all have to say.

I want to thank my amazing husband for his continued support, even if it's me mimicking him and telling me I'm doing a great job.

To my amazing author friends, if it weren't for you...I'd probably still be editing my little heart away!

Also By

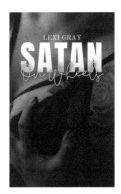

Satan on Wheels by Lexi Gray is a slow-burn, enemies to loves, motorcycle club thriller that you don't want to miss! Action packed full of fan-favorite tropes and triggers!

Don't forget, smut starts on page one! It's book one of the Rubber Down Duology.

Coming Soon

Birdie

Being friends is easy. There's no strings, no weird after math. Just simply coexisting together in a town that will siphon your money for rent alone. Being friends means we can talk about our latest hookups, even if they ended badly. We can talk about our families, our lives, how our day is…everything without complication. Then I opened my eyes. If I had to exist without him, it wouldn't be one worth living. He completes me. Only, I may have waited too long to tell him.

Scout

She's never noticed me. I make a move then get pushed right back into the pit of friendship. I can't tell if it's on purpose, or simply because we've known each other almost all of our lives. We were in diapers together, learned to walk and talk. Even had the same teachers throughout school. She's my world. I wouldn't exist without her. She wonders why I'm so put off by others…I only see her.

You're a woman stuck in a man's world. You had to fight your way to the top with no legacy to follow. You've worked to push through your troubled past, putting it behind you. Of all things you've learned on your road to recovery, you know your self worth. You're hot, you're a motorcycle babe, and you're able to put a bullet between the enemy's eyes without hesitation. You learn to survive, living day to day. You move on...but the past is never really gone. What you didn't expect? Three members of the club waltzing into your life. Enveloping you into a world between pain and pleasure. The pain can sometimes outweigh the pleasure, but can you survive?

Welcome to Leather Dreams.

Milton Keynes UK
Ingram Content Group UK Ltd.
UKHW040646191223
434651UK00001B/72